STAR WARS

BOBA FETT

THE FIGHT TO SURVIVE

TERRY BISSON

LUCAS BOOKS

SCHOLASTIC INC.

New York   Toronto   London   Auckland   Sydney
Mexico City   New Delhi   Hong Kong   Buenos Aires

www.starwars.com
www.starwarskids.com
www.scholastic.com

ISBN 0-439-33927-8

Cover art by Louise Bova

12 11 10 9 8 7 6 5 4 3 2 1   2 3 4 5 6 7/0

Printed in the U.S.A.
First Scholastic printing, May 2002

CHAPTER ONE

Rain.

Some hate it.

Some love it.

Some, like Boba Fett, can hardly remember a time without it.

Supposedly, free water is rare in the galaxy, but you would never know it on his planet. It comes down in sheets, day and night, covering this world, which is all seas except for a few cities on platforms.

The world is called Kamino. The city where Boba and his father live is called Tipoca City.

Lived, rather. For this is the story of how they left, and why, and what happened after that . . .

You may have heard of Boba Fett's father. He was a bounty hunter. The fiercest, fastest, and most fearless bounty hunter in the galaxy.

Boba Fett was the kid standing in his shadow or by his side. Or usually, both.

When he was lucky, that is. When his dad took him along. Which was almost always. Boba was ten, nearly but not quite old enough to be on his own.

Boba liked going with his father. Seeing new worlds, experiencing the cold thrill of hyperspace, and even getting to try his hand at the controls of his father's small but deadly starship, *Slave I*, from time to time.

A bounty hunter is an outlaw, a tracker — and sometimes a killer — for hire. He doesn't care who his targets are, or who they're running from, or why. He works for the highest bidder, which means the richest and the most ruthless beings in the galaxy. No questions asked.

Being a bounty hunter's son means keeping your mouth shut and your eyes open.

No problem. Boba Fett was proud of his father and proud of what he did.

"I'm a bounty hunter's son," he would say to himself proudly. The reason he said it to himself, and to no one else, was that he had no one else to say it to.

He had no friends.

How can you have friends when you live and travel in secret, sneaking on and off planets, avoiding police and security and the dreaded, nosy, Jedi Knights?

A bounty hunter must always be ready to go anywhere and face any danger. That was from Jango Fett's code, the rule by which he lived.

Boba Fett had his own, smaller, more personal code: *A bounty hunter's kid must always be ready to go with him.*

At age ten, Boba had seen more of the galaxy than most grown-ups. What he hadn't seen was the inside of a schoolroom (for he'd never been to school). What he hadn't seen was a mother's smile (for he had no mother). What he hadn't heard was the laughter of a friend (for he had no friends).

Just because he hadn't been to school didn't mean Boba was stupid or ignorant.

There were always books. Books to take on trips; books to read at home on Kamino. He could get all the books he wanted ("Two at a time, only, please!") from the little library at the foot of his street in Tipoca City.

The library was just a slot in a doorway, but when Boba rang the bell the librarian passed out new books and took back the ones that were due, the ones Boba had read (or given up on, or decided were boring).

The librarian, Whrr, was almost like a friend. A friend Boba had never actually seen.

Boba had no idea what Whrr looked like — or even if he was a person. He was just a voice through a slot in the library door. In fact, Boba figured Whrr could be a droid, since he could hear him whirring and clicking when he was getting books or hologames.

Mostly books.

Whrr didn't like hologames. "Use your imagination!" he would say. "Find the pictures there! Find the music there!"

Boba agreed. He liked books because the pictures they made in his mind were better than the ones in the hologames.

Boba knew about friends from books.

Lots of books are about friends. Friends having adventures, making discoveries, or just hanging out.

Sometimes Boba pretended to have friends. (Pretending is a form of wishing.)

But his father's voice was always in his head: "Boba, stay unattached. Remember: *No friends, no enemies. Only allies and adversaries.*"

That saying was from Jango Fett's code. Boba's father had lots of sayings, and they were all from his code.

Jango Fett had one friend, though. She was a bounty hunter herself. Her name was Zam Wesell.

Zam could be beautiful but bad. She *liked* to be bad. She sometimes read books about famous outlaws and bloody battles.

It was Zam who first mentioned that Boba should read, even though she herself didn't read much. "Want adventure? Read books," Zam said. "Then when you get tired of the excitement, you can close the book. Better than real life."

Boba's father didn't read much. "Books? A waste of time," he said. "Read maps, Boba. Instructions. Warnings. Important stuff."

Boba read all that — but he liked books better. Especially books about droids and starships, stuff he knew he could use someday.

Sometimes Boba thought Zam had told him to read books just because his dad thought it was a waste of time. Zam liked to tease Jango.

Zam was a changeling, a Clawdite. She changed the form of her body back and forth, depending on the situation.

Mothers didn't do that, Boba was pretty sure. He had read about mothers in books, even though he had never met one.

A mother seemed like a nice thing to have.

*   *   *

Once, when he was little, Boba asked his father who his mother was.

"You never had one," said his father. "You are a clone. That means you are my son. Period. No one else, no woman was involved."

Boba nodded. That meant he was exactly like his father, Jango Fett. That meant he was special.

Still, sometimes, in secret, he wished he had a mother.

Boba and his father lived on Kamino because Jango Fett had a job to do there. He was training a special army of super-soldiers for a man named Count Tyranus.

Boba liked to watch the soldiers, lined up in long ranks, marching in the rain. They never got tired and they never complained and they all looked exactly alike — exactly like his father, only younger. Exactly like Boba himself, only older.

"They are also my clones," Jango Fett told him once when he was little.

It was what Boba had expected to hear. But it still hurt. "Just like me?"

"Not like you," said Jango Fett. "They are just soldiers. They grow up twice as fast and only live half as long. You are the only true clone. You are my real son."

"I see," said Boba. He felt better. Still, he didn't go watch the clones march anymore. And he didn't feel quite as special as before.

Tyranus was an old man with a long, lean face and eyes like a hawk.

Boba had never seen him in person — only on holograms when he gave instructions to Jango Fett, or asked about the progress of the clone army.

Jango called him "Count" and was always polite. But that didn't mean he liked him, Boba knew.

Always be polite to a client. That was part of Jango's code.

One night Boba heard his father and the Count talking about a new job on a faraway planet.

The Count told Jango Fett that the job would be very dangerous.

That didn't stop Boba's father, of course. Later on, Boba wondered if maybe the Count had played up the danger to make sure Jango took the job.

You never knew, with grown-ups.

Jango agreed to do the job. He told the Count he would have to meet up with Zam Wesell and take her along with him.

Boba grinned when he heard that. If they were both going, that meant he might get to go, too.

No such luck.

The next morning, Jango Fett strapped on his battle armor and told Boba that he and Zam were going on a trip.

"Me too?" Boba asked hopefully.

Jango shook his head. "Sorry, son. You're going to have to stay home alone."

Boba groaned.

"*A bounty hunter never complains,*" said Jango, in that special voice he reserved for his code. "And neither does his son."

"But . . ."

"No buts, son. This is a special job for the Count. Zam and I have to travel fast and light."

"I'm fast," Boba said. "And I'm light!"

Jango Fett laughed. "A little too light," he said, patting Boba on the head. "But big enough to stay here on your own. It will only be a few days."

The next morning Boba woke up alone in the apartment. Home alone — but not entirely alone.

His father had left him a bowl with five sea-mice in it. And a note: *We'll be back when these are gone.*

Sea-mice can live in either air or water. They are incredibly cute, with big brown eyes and little paws that turn to flippers when you put them into the water.

They are also incredibly good to eat . . . if you are a sea eel.

Jango's pet sea eel lived in a tank in the bed-room.

CHAPTER TWO

Boba was surprised to find that he liked being home alone.

The apartment was all his. Three squares came out of the cookslot every day, heated to perfection.

Boba could come and go as he liked. He could hang around the spaceport, admiring the sleek fighters and imagining himself at the controls. He could pretend he was a bounty hunter and "track" unsuspecting people on the street. Or, when he grew tired of the endless rain, he could curl up and read on the couch.

It wasn't even lonely. When Boba was with his father, Jango Fett hardly ever talked. But when Boba was alone he could hear his father's voice in his head all the time. "Boba do this. Boba do that."

It was as good as having him actually around. Better, in fact.

*   *   *

The first two days were easy. And in three more days, Jango and Zam Wesell would be back. How did Boba know?

There were only three sea-mice left. The eel ate one a day. Every morning Boba took a sea-mouse out of the bowl and dropped it into the eel's tank.

The eel had no name. Just "eel."

Boba didn't like its narrow eyes and huge mouth. Or the way it swallowed the little sea-mice in one gulp — then digested them slowly, taking all day.

It was creepy.

Jango Fett usually fed the eel. But now it was Boba's job. The note had said it all: *We'll be back when these are gone.*

Boba knew that his dad thought it was important for his son to learn to do what was necessary, even when it was creepy. Even when it was cruel.

The bounty hunter is free of attachments was one of his sayings. Another was: *Life feeds on death.*

On the third morning, when Boba woke up and heated his breakfast, there were three sea-mice left.

He decided to spare one. He felt sorry for the

sea-mice with their big brown eyes. What if he gave the eel his own breakfast — or, say, half of it?

He could hear his dad's voice in his ear: *Vary your routine. Patterns are traps.* (JFC)

"Okay, Dad," Boba said.

Boba broke his breakfast roll in two and dropped half into the eel's tank. It was gone in an instant.

Then he reached down into the bowl and picked up one of the sea-mice. The sea-mouse made it easy, grabbing Boba's fingers with his tiny paws.

Maybe he knows I'm not going to feed him to the eel, Boba thought. But no, each of the others had looked at him in exactly the same way, right before he had dropped them into the eel's tank.

This one has it right, though, Boba thought. *I have to make him gone, but I can do it another way. I am going to give him his freedom.*

That was the plan, anyway.

Boba took the sea-mouse into the hall, down the turbolift, and out to the courtyard behind the apartment building.

He set him down in the weed garden. "So long, little sea-mouse," he said. "You're free."

The sea-mouse looked up at Boba, more terri-fied than happy. *Maybe he doesn't know what freedom is*, Boba thought. Boba gave him a push with his fingertips, and the tiny creature disappeared into the tall, rain-wet grass. A little wave of movement in the grass showed where he was going.

Then a bigger wave intersected it.

Boba heard a tiny scream — then silence.

CHAPTER THREE

That afternoon Boba went to the library. It always made him feel better to go to the library.

Well, not always, but often.

He stuck the books he was returning into the slot. The light came on, and Whrr whirred and clicked. "Boba!" he said. "How're you feeling?"

"Not great," said Boba. He told Whrr what had happened with the sea-mouse.

"Not great," agreed Whrr, "but at least you tried. Life is hard on the weak and the small, I guess."

"What do you mean, you guess?" asked Boba. "Don't you know?"

"Not really," said Whrr. "That's why I stay in here, out of the way." He whirred his change-the-subject noise. "Ready for some new books? Did you actually finish these?"

"Mostly," said Boba. "I like to read about navigation and starship flying."

"You are reading faster," said Whrr, passing the new books through the slot. "That's good!"

"Why is that good?"

"You can read more books!"

Boba had to laugh.

"Why are you laughing?" Whrr asked. He sounded a little offended.

"My dad says, if you are a pilot, everything looks like a ship," said Boba.

"So?"

"So, Whrr, if you had your way, everybody would read books."

"So? I don't understand what's so funny about that," Whrr said, with a disapproving click.

"Never mind, see ya later!" Boba said, and he took his books and ran.

Time to get rid of another sea-mouse.

Boba woke up determined to try to do the right thing this time. He gave the eel all his breakfast. The eel ate it in one gulp.

There were only two sea-mice left in the bowl. They both looked up at him with their little brown eyes pleading.

"I have to make you gone," Boba said as he picked one up. "But I'm not going to feed you to the eel. I'm going to set you free for real."

He locked the apartment door and took the turbolift down to the street. He stuck the sea-mouse inside his shirt so no one could see it.

It seemed to like it there. When Boba pulled it out it was sleeping.

He held it out in the rain as he walked toward the edge of Tipoca City. He wanted to watch its paw turn into a flipper, but it only turned halfway.

I guess it takes seawater, Boba thought, heading toward the sound of the waves.

Tipoca City is built on a platform over the sea. Huge waves boom and bang and crash, day and night. Kamino is called the "Planet of Storms."

Boba hung onto the railing and leaned over the edge of the platform. He looked down, waiting for a lull in the waves.

Finally, there it was — a long green stretch of smooth water. It looked perfect for a little sea-mouse!

"You're free, little buddy," Boba said as he dropped the tiny creature into the water. The sea-mouse stared up as it fell, as if it wanted one last look at its benefactor, its protector, the great giant Boba who had rescued it from its bowl. . . .

It hit the water with a little *plunk*.

Then Boba saw a dark shape in the water, and a flash of teeth from below.

And the sea-mouse was gone.

Not even a stain on the water was left.

Boba spent the rest of the day playing hologames and staring out the window into the rain. He was tired of books. He was tired of reading about happy families and kids with friends. And pets.

He was tired of being home alone.

He missed Zam's jokes (even the dumb ones). He missed his father's sayings (even the ones he had heard a million times).

The next morning he picked up the last seamouse out of the bowl. "Sorry, buddy," he said as he dropped it into the eel's tank. "It's just the way the world works."

Then he sat down to eat his own breakfast and wait for his father and Zam to get home.

CHAPTER FOUR

All day Boba was excited, waiting for a certain sound.

Or a bunch of sounds.

Finally, late in the afternoon, there they were: a symphony of little clicks and clacks, all coming from the locks that hung on the apartment door.

Then the door slid open, and there was Jango Fett, looking strong and bold in his Mandalorian battle armor, standing in a puddle of rainwater in the hall.

"Dad!" Boba said. "Where's Zam?"

"Later," his father said.

Jango Fett took off his battle armor and laid it out on the floor of the bedroom while Boba watched. He called it "the suit." He was much smaller without it.

Jango's face under the helmet was sad and grooved with old scars. The face on his helmet was ruthless and cruel. Boba never wondered which was his father's "real" face. Both were real to him: the worried father, the fearless warrior.

"Where's Zam?" Boba asked again.

"Why are you asking all these questions, son?"

"I have a joke to tell her." He didn't really, but he figured he could always think of one.

"You'll have to save it for somebody else."

Somebody else? There wasn't anybody else! But Boba knew better than to argue with his father.

"Okay," he said. He hung his head to hide his disappointment and started to leave the room. He could tell his father wanted to be alone.

"Zam won't be around anymore," Jango said.

Boba stopped at the door. "Ever?"

"Ever," said Jango.

Only the way he said it, it sounded like *never*.

When Jango Fett wasn't wearing the Mandalorian battle armor, he wore regular clothes. Without the helmet, few recognized him as Jango Fett, the bounty hunter.

The armor was old and scarred, like Jango Fett himself. He always took it off and cleaned it after returning from a job, but he never polished it. He left the scratches alone.

"You don't want it to shine," he told Boba as they worked together cleaning the armor later that afternoon. *"Never call attention to yourself."*

"Yes, sir," Boba said.

Jango Fett's face seemed even sadder and older than usual. Boba wondered if it had to do with Zam.

Finally he got up the courage to ask.

"She was about to betray us," Jango said. "It couldn't be allowed. There are penalties. She would have done the same if it were me."

Boba didn't understand. What was his father trying to tell him? "Did something bad happen to Zam?"

Jango nodded slowly. "Being a bounty hunter means you don't always make it home. Someday the inevitable will happen. And when it does . . ."

"What does *inevitable* mean?" Boba asked.

"Inevitable means a sure thing. Death is a sure thing."

Suddenly Boba got it. "Zam is dead, isn't she, Dad?"

Jango nodded.

Boba fought back tears. "How — how did it happen?"

"You don't want to know."

Boba felt sadness wash over him like a wave. Followed by a colder wave of fear. If it could happen to Zam, could it happen to his father?

Boba didn't want to think about that. His dad was right: He didn't want to know.

After he had finished helping his father clean the battle armor and reload the weapons systems, Boba went out and walked all the way down to the end of the street and back.

Zam, dead. No more dumb jokes. No more bright laughter. Boba Fett's lonely world had just gotten even lonelier.

Kamino is a good planet for feeling sad because it's always raining. When you've been in the rain, nobody can tell you've been crying.

When Boba got back to the apartment, he saw that his father had been walking in the rain, too.

Funny, thought Boba. *I didn't see him out there.*

After supper, Jango Fett said, "Boba, listen up."

Boba listened up.

"What happened to Zam could happen to any of us. To any bounty hunter. Do you understand?"

Boba nodded — but his nod was a lie. He was determined *not* to understand. He had promised himself *not* to think about it. He couldn't imagine it, anyway. Who or what could get the best of his father in a fight?

"Good," said Jango Fett. "So, son, I want you to take this."

Jango handed Boba a book.

Boba was shocked. *My dad?! A book?!*

Jango seemed to know what Boba was thinking. "It's not a book, son," he said. "It's a message unit, from me. For you, when the time comes."

Not a book? It looked like an ordinary book, about two fingers thick, with a hard cover. It was black, with nothing on the cover. No words, no pictures. Nothing, front or back.

Boba tried to open it but the pages seemed stuck together. He pulled harder on the cover, and his father shook his head.

"Don't open it," Jango said. "Because when you open it, your childhood will be over. And it is too soon for that. I want you to have what I never had: a childhood."

Boba nodded. Though he was confused. Why had his father given him a book if he didn't want him to open it?

Then his father told him:

"If something happens to me, you should open it. It will tell you what you need to know. Who to ask for. Who to avoid. What to do. What not. Until then, keep it closed, and keep it hidden. Understand, son?"

Boba nodded. He tossed the black book (that was not really a book) into the pile with his library books. He wasn't going to need it. Ever. No way. Like, something bad was going to happen to his father, the fiercest, fastest, most fearless bounty hunter in the galaxy?

No way. Unthinkable. Which simply meant that Boba was *not* going to think about it.

CHAPTER FIVE

The next day, Boba and his father went fishing. The rain was light, so they sat on a rock at the edge of the sea. Boba took potshots at rollerfish with his pocker, a laser-aimed spear-thrower. Jango made him turn the laser off and sight by eye.

Boba knew that the fishing trip was his father's way of trying to make him feel better, so he'd forget about Zam's death. Boba did his best to concentrate.

He kept on fishing even when Taun We, one of the Kaminoans, stopped by to talk with Jango. She was tall and white, like a root that has just been pulled out of the ground. Her dark eyes were as big as saucers, her neck long and thin.

Boba usually liked Taun We, but today it was business, business, business. Something about the clones. Boba tried not to listen. He didn't want to hear about the clone army — his ten thousand twin brothers. It made him feel creepy just thinking about it.

He was glad when Taun We left, and to prove

it, he speared a few more rollerfish. He tried to act excited to please his dad, but the fun had gone out of it.

Boba couldn't stop thinking about the clones.

He couldn't stop thinking about Zam.

Boba *did* get excited again, though, when they passed the spaceport on their way back to the apartment. There was a new ship on the landing pad. It was a sleek starfighter he had only seen in pictures before.

"Wow!" he said. "It's a Delta-7!"

"And what of the droid?" Jango asked, pointing to the nav unit behind the cockpit.

"It's an R4-P," said Boba excitedly. While his father listened, he listed the starfighter's features. Extra armaments, extra speed — the Delta-7 with the R4-P was the kind of ship only a few, select pilots could handle.

"Like who?" Jango asked.

"Like you!" Boba said as they hurried home in the rain. He was happy to show off what he had learned from his reading. And even happier to bring a smile to his father's face.

But the smile didn't last. Jango seemed thoughtful. Preoccupied. Even worried.

He went into the bedroom to take a nap while Boba sat down with a reference — *Starfighters of the Galaxy.* He was curious to know how such a sleek ship as the Delta-7 had found its way to out-of-the-way Kamino, where nothing important or exciting ever happened.

Boba had barely started to read when he heard the door buzz. He and his father didn't have any friends, especially with Zam gone, so he was surprised.

It was Taun We again. And this time she wasn't alone. The man standing next to her wore a simple robe and no jewelry. Under his robe Boba could see the outline of a lightsaber.

A Jedi.

All of a sudden, Boba knew where the star-fighter had come from.

Cautiously, he opened the door.

"Boba, is your father here?" Taun We asked.

"Yes."

Say no more than necessary. That was a favorite saying of Jango Fett. And Boba knew that it especially applied when the Jedi were around.

"May we see him?"

The Jedi said nothing. Just stood there, watching and listening. Cool and collected. But also a little scary.

Boba tried to be cool himself. "Sure," he said.

Always be polite. Especially to your enemies.

And the Jedi, as keepers of the peace, were the natural enemies of bounty hunters, who operated outside the law.

Boba stepped back to let them in. The Jedi was looking around as if he had never been in an apartment before. *Nosy!* Boba thought. He decided to ignore him.

"Dad! Taun We's here!"

Jango Fett came out of the bedroom. He looked at both of the visitors, and he didn't seem to like what he saw.

"Welcome back, Jango," Taun We said, pretending she hadn't just seen him. "Was your trip productive?"

"Fairly."

Boba listened carefully. Taun We was sounding friendly, as usual. Meanwhile his father was looking the Jedi up and down. To say that Jango didn't seem to like what he saw would be obvious, like saying Kamino is rainy. It was more than that.

Boba wondered if they had met before. He wondered if the Jedi had anything to do with the death of Zam.

"This is Jedi Master Obi-Wan Kenobi," Taun We said. "He's come to check on our progress."

"That right?" Jango said.

The two men stared at each other. It was like a battle fought without words or weapons.

Boba watched, fascinated. It was obvious to him that his father could have whipped the stupid

Jedi with one finger. But something was holding him back.

"Your clones are very impressive," said the Jedi with a slight bow. "You must be very proud."

"I'm just a simple man," Jango Fett said, bowing back. "Trying to make my way in the universe."

"Aren't we all?" said the Jedi.

It was like a fight to see who could be most polite!

Meanwhile, the Jedi was looking into the bedroom, where the Mandalorian battle helmet and armor were lying on the floor.

Jango moved in front of the door to block the Jedi's view.

"Ever make your way as far into the interior as Coruscant?" the Jedi asked.

"Once or twice," Jango answered coolly.

"Recently?"

This is one very nosy Jedi! Boba thought. He wondered why his father was talking to him at all.

"Possibly," said Jango, and Boba knew from the tone of the answer that his father *had* been to Coruscant.

And the Jedi knew it, too.

Now Boba knew for sure that the Jedi and Jango had encountered each other before, and that the Jedi had had something to do with Zam's death. How he hated the Jedi's smug little smile!

"Then you must know Master Sifo-Dyas," the Jedi said.

"Boba, close the door," said Jango in Huttese, a language they both knew well.

Boba did what his father asked, never taking his eyes off the Jedi. He wanted him to feel his hate.

Meanwhile Jango Fett was fencing. Using words instead of a sword to block the Jedi's moves. "Master who?" he asked.

"Sifo-Dyas. Isn't he the Jedi who hired you for this job?"

"Never heard of him," said Jango.

"Really!?" said the Jedi. For the first time, he looked surprised.

"I was recruited by a man called Tyranus," said Jango. "On one of the moons of Bogden."

"No? I thought . . ."

Taun We stepped in then. "Sifo-Dyas told us to expect him," she said to the Jedi, pointing to Boba's father. "And he showed up just when your Jedi Master said he would. We have kept the Jedi's involvement a secret until your arrival, just as your Master requested."

The Jedi seemed surprised by all this. And trying not to show it. "Curious," he said.

"Do you like your army?" Jango Fett asked. His cold smile seemed to Boba like a sword thrust straight toward the nosy Jedi's heart.

"I look forward to seeing them in action," said the Jedi. A pretty good parry, Boba had to admit.

"They'll do their job well, I'll guarantee that," said Jango.

The Jedi gave up. "Thanks for your time, Jango."

"Always a pleasure to meet a Jedi," said Boba's father with a slight, sarcastic smile.

The door slid shut and the locks began to snap closed. Boba was thrilled. After winning an encounter like that, he figured his father would looked pleased, even triumphant. Instead, Jango Fett's face was creased with lines of worry, and he seemed deep in thought.

Boba began to wonder if his father had really won the battle. "What is it, Dad?" he asked.

"Pack your things," Jango said. "We're getting out of here for a while."

CHAPTER SIX

While Jango Fett put his battle armor on, Boba threw everything the two owned (which wasn't much) into an expandable flight bag.

"Get a move on, Boba!"

Boba knew his father wasn't afraid of anything. But after the encounter with the strange Jedi, Jango seemed nervous. Worried. Not frightened, but . . . *concerned*, at least.

And he was in a BIG hurry.

After he had filled the bag, Boba threw all the dirty dishes into the cleaning slot. He didn't have to be neat at all. If it hadn't been so scary, it would have been fun.

"Leave the rest," Jango said. "We don't have time."

Be careful what you wish for! How many times had Boba dreamed of having time away from stormy Kamino and living somewhere else, with sunshine — and maybe even friends?

Now it was happening. The having time away part, anyway. Boba was glad, and yet . . .

There was the bed where he had slept and

dreamed. The windowsill where he had sat and read and watched the endless rain. The box where he had kept his books, clothes, and old toys, all in one pile.

It's hard to leave the only place you've ever lived, especially when you don't know when you'll be back. It's like leaving behind little pieces of yourself. It's like . . .

Boba caught himself. This was no time to get sentimental. His father was in a hurry. They had to get going.

And there was one last thing he had to do before leaving Tipoca City.

"Whoa! Where are you going?" Jango asked. His battle armor was on, helmet and all. He was holding what looked like a whip. "Where are you taking that stuff?"

"Uh, Dad . . . library books?"

Boba hoped his father would understand that he had to return them. Who knew when they were coming back? And Boba didn't want Whrr to be charging him for overdue books.

"Make it fast, son," Jango said. "And while you're at it —"

He handed Boba the "whip." It was the eel. "Turn him loose in the sea. Let him try feeding himself for a change."

"Yes, sir!" Boba was out the door before his father could change his mind. The eel was coiled around one arm, and he carried the books in the other.

He ran through the rain as fast as he could. He stopped at the edge of the platform where he had taken the sea-mouse. He leaned over the railing and dropped the eel into the waves.

Plunk.

Boba saw a dark shape, a flash of teeth. And the eel was gone.

"Good riddance!" he muttered as he ran toward the library. "Life is hard for the small and the weak. And it's all relative."

Boba hurriedly shoved the books into the slot. One, two, three . . .

Whrr whirred happily. "How about this batch?" he asked from behind the door, in his tinny voice. "What did you think? Any good?"

"Not too bad," Boba said. "But I don't have time to talk now."

"No? Why not? Don't you want to check out some more books?"

Usually Boba liked talking about books. But today there was no time. "Have to go!" he said. "So long!"

"Hurry back, Boba," Whrr said. "But wait, here's . . ."

"No time to wait!" Boba didn't have the heart to tell his friend that he didn't know when he would be coming back.

So he just turned and ran.

Jango Fett, fierce looking in his full battle armor, was waiting with the flight bag in front of the apartment. Boba could tell his father was mad at him for taking so long. But neither of them said anything.

The two walked quickly to the tiny landing pad where *Slave I*, the bounty hunter's small, swift starship, was parked. Jango stowed the bags while Boba checked out the ship for takeoff.

Boba had just completed the preflight "walk-around" when he heard footsteps. At first he thought it might be Taun We, coming to say goodbye.

No such luck.

It was the Jedi, Obi-Wan Kenobi. The one who had been at the apartment asking all the questions.

And he was running.

"Stop!" he shouted.

Yeah, right! thought Boba.

Jango clearly had the same thought. He drew his blaster and fired, while ordering, "Boba, get on board!"

Boba didn't have to be told twice. He got into the cockpit and watched as his father fired up his battle armor's jet-pack and rocketed to the top of a nearby building. There, Jango Fett knelt and began to fire down at the Jedi with his blaster rifle.

KA-WHAP!

KA-WHAP!

Though he had never flown *Slave I* alone, Boba knew all the controls and weapons systems by heart. Reaching over his head, he switched the main systems on, so the ship would be ready to go when his father got through whipping the Jedi.

Then he got an even better idea. He activated the blaster cannon controls.

Boba had practiced this so many times, he knew just how to do it. He got the Jedi in the sights and pressed FIRE.

SKA-PLANG!

A hit! Or almost.

The Jedi was thrown violently to the ground, his lightsaber knocked out of his hand. Boba was about to fire again and finish him off when his father got in the way.

Jango rocketed down from the building and stood face-to-face with the Jedi.

The Jedi charged.

Jango charged back.

Cool! thought Boba. He had never seen his father in hand-to-hand combat before, and it was awesome.

The Jedi's mysterious Force was no match for Jango Fett's Mandalorian body armor. The Jedi was losing — badly. He got desperate and made a grab, but Jango used his jet-pack to blast up and kick him away.

"Go!" shouted Boba, even though he knew no one could hear.

The Jedi fell and slid toward the edge of the landing pad, where it projected out over the crashing waves. He seemed to be using his so-called Force to get his lightsaber back, but Jango Fett spoiled that plan. From his wrist gauntlet, he shot out a restraining wire, which wrapped around the Jedi's wrists.

Then Jango fired up his jet-pack again, dragging the Jedi toward the edge of the platform — and the water.

"Go, Dad!" Boba shouted.

But the Jedi was able to catch the wire on a column. It stopped his slide and pulled him to his feet. Then he yanked on the wire. . . .

SPROINNGG!!

Jango hit the platform, hard. His jet-pack flared, spat . . . and exploded.

BARRRROOOM!

Oh, no! Boba saw the whole thing. He tried to get a shot with the laser, but now both men were sliding toward the edge of the platform — and the huge waves crashing below.

"Dad!" Boba yelled. "Dad!" He banged on the cockpit canopy, as if his fists and his cries could somehow stop his father's slide toward certain death —

But it wasn't over yet. Jango Fett ejected the wire from his wrist gauntlet, freeing himself. Then he used the gripping claws built into his battle armor to stop his slide at the last instant.

Meanwhile, the Jedi slid right over the edge.

Boba fell back in his seat, shaking with relief: His father was safe. And triumph: The Jedi was gone!

Over the edge. Into the sea.

Good riddance! Boba thought.

The ramp was opening.

Boba scrambled out of the pilot's seat just in time.

His father leaped into the seat. The engines roared to life, and the starship lifted off into the storm, which was raging all around.

Boba looked down at the waves. There was no sign of the Jedi, and no wonder. Who could swim in that stupid robe? It had dragged him under, for sure.

"Life is hard for the small and the weak!" Boba said under his breath, and they hurtled upward, into the clouds.

"What, Boba?"

"I said, 'Good going, Dad!'"

CHAPTER SEVEN

Boba had been in space before, traveling with his father. But when you are real little, you don't notice a lot.

Now that he was ten, he understood what he was seeing. Everything looked new and exciting.

On Kamino it was almost always cloudy. The clouds were gray on the bottom, and black as night on the inside. But from above, they were as white as the snow Boba had seen in vids and read about in books.

The sky above was bright, bright blue.

Then, as *Slave I* rose higher and higher, the sky grew darker — blue-black, then inky black. Then Boba saw something even more beautiful than the clouds.

Stars.

Boba knew what they were, of course. He had read about the stars; he had seen them in vids and pictures, and observed them personally on trips with his father to other planets. Yet he had never really paid attention. Little kids don't notice things that are *that* far away. And the stars were almost never visible from cloudy Kamino, even at night. But now he was ten, and now . . .

Boba saw a million stars, each light-years away.

"Wow," he said.

"What is it, Boba?" his father asked.

Boba didn't know what to say. The galaxy was made of a million suns, burning fiercely. Around each sun were planets, each made of a million rocks and stones, and each stone was made of millions of atoms, and . . .

"It's the galaxy," Boba said. "Why is there . . . ?"

"Why is there what, Boba?"

"Why is there so much of it?"

Jango Fett let his son "fly" *Slave I*, which meant just sitting in the pilot's seat while the autopilot flew the ship. He was busy fitting his battle armor with a new jet-pack to replace the one that had blown up in the fight with the Jedi.

When he was done, he got into the pilot's seat, and Boba asked, "Are we moving to another world, Dad?"

"For now."

"Which one?"

"You'll see."

"Why?"

"Why are you asking so many questions?"

That was Boba's signal to shut up. His father

had his reasons for everything, but he usually kept them to himself.

"You don't want to know," Jango Fett said as he hit the button marked HYPERSPACE.

If space was awesome, hyperspace was double awesome.

Double awesome strange.

As soon as *Slave I* shifted into lightspeed and slipped into hyperspace, Boba's head started to spin. The stars were flying past like raindrops. It was like a dream, with far and near twisted together, time and space mixed like oil and water, in swirls.

Boba dozed off, because even strange becomes tiring when *everything* is strange. . . .

Boba dreamed he was meeting the mother he had never had. He was at a big reception in a palace, and he was alone. It was like a story in a book. There was someone coming toward him, making her way through the crowd. She was beautiful, in a white dress. She was walking toward Boba, faster and faster, and her smile was as bright as . . .

"Boba?"

"Yes!?"

"Wake up, son."

Boba opened his eyes and saw his father at the controls of *Slave I*. They were out of hyperspace, back in "normal," three-dimensional space.

They were floating. Directly ahead of them was a huge red planet with orange rings.

It was beautiful, but not as beautiful as the vision Boba had seen in his dream, coming toward him across the ballroom floor. Not as beautiful as . . . Boba felt himself slipping back into his dream.

"Geonosis," said Jango Fett.

"What?" Boba sat up.

"Name of the planet. Geonosis."

As *Slave I* approached Geonosis, it headed toward the rings. Only from a distance were they smooth and beautiful. Up close, Boba could see that the rings were made out of asteroids and meteors, lumps of rock and ice — space rubble.

Up close they were dangerous and ugly.

Jango's hands were dancing over the starship's controls, switching them from autopilot to manual. Flying under the rings would be tricky. As he expertly eased the ship into approach orbit, he said, "Next time, when we get to a planet that's easier to land on, I'll let you fly the approach on your own, son."

"Really, Dad? Does that mean I'm old enough?"

Jango patted his son on the shoulder. "Just about, Boba. Just about."

Boba leaned back, smiling. Life was better than dreams. Who needed a mom when you had a dad like Jango Fett?

Suddenly Boba caught a glimpse of something on the rear vid screen. A blip. "Dad, I think we're being tracked!"

Jango's smile disappeared. The blip was matching their every turn. A ship on their tail.

"Look at the sensor screen," Boba said excitedly. "Isn't that a cloaking shadow?"

Jango switched the sensor screen to higher res. It showed a tracker attached to the hull of *Slave I*.

Boba couldn't believe it. Hadn't he watched the Jedi slide into the stormy sea of Kamino? How could the Jedi have survived to follow them?

"He must have put a tracking device on our hull during the fight," said Jango, with the steel of determination in his voice. "We'll fix that!"

Boba was just about to ask *how*, when his dad pushed him back into his seat.

"Hang on, son. We'll move into the asteroid field. He won't be able to follow us there. If he does, we'll leave him a couple of surprises."

CHAPTER EIGHT

Into the asteroid field! Boba felt a cold touch of fear as his father pulled back on the controls and *Slave I* slid upward, into the ring itself.

Jagged rocks zipped past, on either side. It was like flying through a forest of stone.

Boba couldn't look. And he couldn't not look, either. He knew that if they hit one, they were dead.

Obliterated.

Erased.

They wouldn't even leave a ripple on the galaxy.

Then Boba told himself: *Stop worrying. Look who's at the controls!*

Boba kept his eyes on his father. The asteroids were still zipping past *Slave I* but they didn't seem quite as scary.

Jango Fett was at the controls.

Boba relaxed and checked the rear viewscreen. "He's gone," he told his father.

"He must have gone on toward the surface," Jango replied.

Suddenly the image on the viewscreen wavered with a rogue signal. In the static Boba saw a familiar outline.

The Delta-7.

"Look, Dad, he's back!"

Jango calmly hit a button on the weaponry console marked SONIC CHARGE: RELEASE.

Boba looked back and saw a canister drifting toward the Jedi starfighter.

He grinned. So long! The Jedi was doomed. . . .

And so was Boba. Because when he turned back around in his seat and looked forward, he saw nothing but stone. *Slave I* was heading straight for a huge, jagged asteroid!

"Dad! Watch out!"

Jango's voice was quiet and cold as he pulled *Slave I* into a steep climb, barely missing the killer rock. "Stay calm, son. We'll be fine. That Jedi won't be able to follow us through this."

That was the plan, anyway. But the Jedi had other ideas. As his father deftly guided *Slave I* through the asteroid field, Boba kept his eyes on the rear screen.

"There he is!" he cried.

The Jedi starfighter was still there, right on their tail. It was as if it were tied to *Slave I.*

Jango shook his head grimly. "He doesn't seem

to be able to take a hint. Well, if we can't lose him, we'll have to finish him."

Hitting a button, he turned the starship and headed straight toward another asteroid, even bigger than the last one.

Only this time, he didn't pull up. Instead, he flew straight toward the jagged surface.

Boba couldn't believe it. Was his own father trying to kill them both? "Watch out!" he cried.

He closed his eyes, waiting for the explosion. *So this is what it's like to die*, he thought. He felt amazingly calm. He wondered how badly it would hurt when they hit. Or would it just be like a flash of light? Or . . .

Or nothing.

With Jango Fett at the controls, *Slave I* never slowed, never hesitated.

It looked like certain death.

The ship dove straight down into a narrow canyon on the asteroid's surface.

At the bottom was a cave, with an opening just big enough for a small starship turned on its side.

Just barely big enough . . .

*   *   *

Something was wrong.

Nothing had happened. Boba was still alive.

He opened his eyes.

He saw rock everywhere. His dad had flown full speed into a hole in the asteroid, and now *Slave I* was speeding through a narrow, winding tunnel.

But going slower and slower.

At least we're still alive, thought Boba. *But if the Jedi is chasing us, why are we slowing down?*

He soon found out. The tunnel went all the way through the asteroid. When *Slave I* emerged from the stone passage, it was right behind the Jedi starfighter.

The hunted had become the hunter. *Slave I* was on the Jedi's tail.

It was the coolest maneuver Boba had ever imagined. He could hardly control his excitement.

"Get him, Dad! Get him! Fire!"

Boba didn't have to tell his father. Jango Fett was already blasting away. On every side of the Jedi starfighter deadly lasers were stitching streaks of light through the blackness of space.

"You got him!" Boba cried, when he saw the Jedi starfighter rocked by an explosion.

A near-miss, but not a kill.

Not yet.

"We'll just have to finish him!" said Jango. He reached up to the weaponry console and, with two quick flicks of his wrist, hit two switches:

TORPEDO: ARM

and then

TORPEDO: RELEASE

It was *Slave I*'s turn to rock as the torpedo kicked out of the hull and locked onto the Jedi starfighter.

Boba watched, fascinated. The Jedi was good, he had to admit. He zigged, he zagged, he tried every kind of evasive maneuver.

But the torpedo was locked on, and closing.

Then the Jedi starfighter flew straight into the path of a huge, tumbling asteroid —

And it was all over.

There was no way to avoid the collision. Caught between the torpedo's blast and the unforgiving stone, the Jedi starfighter disappeared. Only a trail of debris remained.

"Got him . . ." Boba breathed. "Yeaaaah!"

Jango's reaction was more subdued. "We won't see him again," he said quietly as he guided the ship out of the asteroids and put it into a descent pattern, down toward the giant red planet.

CHAPTER NINE

Boba had thought Geonosis might be different from Kamino, with schools, other kids, and lots to do.

It was different, all right, but that was all.

On Kamino it rained all the time; on Geonosis it hardly ever rained. Kamino was all sea; Geonosis was a sea of red sand, with big rock towers called stalagmites sticking up like spikes, here and there, from the sandy desert.

In fact, the planet looked deserted. At least that's what Boba thought when he first arrived.

Jango Fett landed *Slave I* on a ledge on the side of one of the stalagmites, or rock towers.

Are we going to camp here on this rock? wondered Boba as the ship settled on its landing struts and the engines died.

Then a door in the stone slid open, and Maintenance Droids appeared to service the ship.

Boba was wide-eyed as he followed his father through the doorway, which turned out to be the entrance to a vast underground city, with long corridors and huge rooms, all connected and lighted with glow tubes, echoing with footsteps and shouts.

Yet it still seemed empty. The only inhabitants were hurrying, distant shadows. No one greeted them; no one even noticed a ten-year-old tagging along after his father.

As they climbed the stairs toward the apartment they had been temporarily assigned, Jango explained to his son that the Geonosians themselves were drones who worked all the time. Their planet was a manufacturing center for Battle Droids. "And the people who make the droids aren't much smarter or more interesting than the droids themselves," Jango said.

"So why are we here?" Boba asked.

"Business," said Jango Fett. "*He who hires my hand . . .*"

"*. . . hires my whole self,*" finished Boba, grinning up at his dad.

"Right," said Jango. He rumpled his son's hair and smiled down at him. "I'm very proud of you, son. You're growing up to be a bounty hunter, just like your old man."

The apartment was high in the stone tower, overlooking the desert. Jango went off to meet with his employer, leaving Boba with a stern warning: "Be here when I get back."

After a couple of hours alone in the apartment, Boba knew that his first impressions had been right. Geonosis was boring. Even more boring than Kamino.

Boredom is kind of like a microscope. It can make little things look big. Boba counted all the stones in the walls of the apartment. He counted all the cracks in the floor.

Bored with cracks and stones, he stared out the narrow window, watching the dust storms roll across the plains and watching the rings wheel across the sky above.

Boba wished he had brought some books. The only one he had was the black book his father had given him, the one he couldn't open. It was in a box with his clothes and old toys, not even worth looking for.

He'd have to make his own excitement. But how?

Be here when I get back. That didn't mean he couldn't leave the apartment. Just that he couldn't go very far.

Boba stepped out into the hallway, closing the door behind him. The stone corridor was dim and quiet. In the distance Boba could hear a booming noise. It sounded almost like the sea on stormy Kamino.

Could there be an ocean here, on this desert planet?

Boba walked to the end of the corridor and stuck his head around the corner. The booming was louder. Now it sounded like a distant drum.

Around the corner there was a stone stairway, leading down. At the bottom the stairs, another hall. At the end of the hall, another stairway.

Stone steps, leading down, into the darkness. Boba followed them, feeling his way, one step at a time. The farther he went, the darker it got.

The darker it got, the louder the booming. It sounded like a giant beating a drum.

Boba had the feeling he had gone too far, but he didn't want to turn back. Not yet. Not until he had discovered what was making the booming noise.

Then a last, long spiral staircase ended in a narrow hallway. The hallway ended at a heavy door. The booming was so loud that the door itself was shaking.

Boba was almost afraid to look. He was about to turn back. Then, in his mind, he heard his father's voice: *Do that which you fear most, and you will find the courage you seek.*

Boba pulled the door open.

BOOM

BOOM

BOOM

There was no wild ocean storm, no giant beating a drum. But Boba was not disappointed. What he saw was even more amazing.

He was looking into a vast underground room, lighted by glowing lamps, and filled with moving shapes. As his eyes adjusted to the dim light, he could see a long assembly line, where huge metal machines were stamping out arms and legs, wheels and blades, heads and torsos. The noise was thunderous. The heavy, rust-colored parts, once stamped, were carried on clattering belts to a central area, where they were assembled by grim-faced Geonosians into warlike Battle Droids, which snapped to attention as soon as their heads were screwed on.

The assembled droids then marched in long lines out of the cavern, through a high, arched doorway, into the darkness.

Boba watched, fascinated. What was the purpose of all these weapons of war? It was hard to believe that there was room in the galaxy for so many Battle Droids and droidekas bristling with blades and blasters.

He imagined them all in action, fighting one another. It was exciting to think about — and a little scary, too.

"Hey, you there!"

Boba looked up. A Security Droid was hurrying his way, across a cartwalk toward the open door.

Rather than explain who he was and what he was doing, Boba decided to do the sensible thing.

He slammed the door and ran.

Be here when I get back, Jango had said. Boba was just shutting the apartment door behind him when he heard footsteps in the hall outside.

Barely made it! thought Boba as his father opened the door.

Two men were with him. One of them was a Geonosian, wearing the elaborate finery of a high official over its branchlike body and barrel-shaped head. The other was more simply dressed, but somehow familiar.

"And so you see, Count Dooku, we have made great progress," said the Geonosian.

It was the *Count* that did it. Boba recognized the other man. "Isn't that Count Tyranus?" Boba asked his father, who was hanging up his battle helmet beside the door.

"Sssshhhhh," said Jango. "We are the only ones who know him by that name."

"Ah, so this is the young one?" the Count said. "You'll be a great bounty hunter someday."

He patted Boba on the head. The gesture was affectionate but the hand was cold, and Boba felt a chill.

"Yes, sir," he said, pulling away.

His father shot him a stern, disapproving look as the three men walked into the apartment's kitchen for their conference.

Boba felt ashamed. He had been rude. The chill must have been his imagination. Count Tyranus was Jango Fett's main employer. Boba owed him not only respect, but trust.

You'll be a great bounty hunter someday. The Count's words rang in Boba's head. He hoped someday they would come true.

His father's battle helmet was hanging by the door. Boba took it down and carried it into the bedroom.

He wanted to see what it looked like from inside. He wanted to feel how it felt to be Jango Fett.

He shut the door behind him and pulled the helmet over his head. He opened his eyes and —

"Wow!"

Boba had expected it to be dark inside the helmet, but it wasn't. There were all sorts of displays scrolling down the inside of the faceplate. Most of them were for weapons and survival systems:

ROCKET DARTS
SONIC BEAM

WRIST GAUNTLET
JET-PACK
BOOT SPIKES
COMLINK
RANGEFINDER

It was like being in the control room of a very small, compact, efficient ship. But it was too heavy. Boba could hardly move his head. He was just lifting it off when —

Click.

Boba heard the bedroom door open. Uh-oh. Now he was in big trouble!

But no — Jango Fett was laughing as he lifted the helmet off Boba's head. "Don't worry, son, your own armor will fit you better."

Boba looked up into his father's eyes. "My own?"

"When you are older," Jango said. "This battle armor was given to me by the Mandalores. You will have your own someday, when you become a bounty hunter."

"And you will teach me to use it?" Boba asked.

"When that day comes, I may not be there," Jango said. "You may be on your own."

"But . . ."

"No buts," said Jango. He attempted a smile. "Don't worry. Your time is yet to come."

He reached out and patted Boba on the head.

This time, there was no chill.

*   *   *

Later that night, Boba heard a strange noise. It was not the booming he had heard before. It was not his father's snores, which came from the next bed.

OOWOOOO!

It was something far away and incredibly lonely.

He went to the narrow window and looked out. The night on Geonosis was as bright as day had been on cloudy Kamino. The planet's orange rings shed a soft light over the desert sands.

There was a red mesa right below the stalagmite city. It was crisscrossed with faint trails that glittered, as if they were paved with diamonds.

The mesa looked interesting but it was strictly off-limits. Jango Fett had said that there were fierce beasts called massiffs that prowled the rocks and cliffs.

OOWOOOO!

There it was again — that lonesome, mournful howl. *A massiff,* thought Boba. It sounded more forlorn than fierce.

He knew the feeling.

He wanted to howl back.

CHAPTER TEN

When Boba woke up, his father was gone. On the table there was breakfast and a note: *Be here when I get back.*

Boba was out the door.

He heard the distant booming but he went the other way, down to the landing platform. *Slave I* was no longer the only starship. It looked tiny compared to the others, which came in all shapes and sizes, but were mostly bigger.

Boba made sure no one was looking, then climbed up the ramp into the cockpit of *Slave I.* The seat was a little low, but other than that, it felt right. He had already memorized the flight controls for both space and atmosphere. He already knew the weapons systems, the multiple lasers and torpedoes. His dad had taught him most of it, and he had figured out the rest for himself.

Boba knew how to start the ship, program the navcomputer, and engage the hyperdrive. He was sure that before long his father would let him try a complete takeoff and landing. He wanted to be ready.

He imagined he was piloting the ship while his father was mowing down his enemies with the laser.

"*Beware the wrath of the Fetts!*" he cried in triumph as he zigged and zagged through the enemy fighters. . . .

"Hey —"

Boba sat up — he must have fallen asleep! He must have been dreaming.

"Hey, kid!"

It was a Geonosian guard.

"It's okay," Boba said. "It's my dad's ship."

He got out of *Slave I* and closed the ramp.

The Geonosian had a stupid but amiable expression.

"How come there's nothing to do around here?" Boba asked, just to be friendly.

The Geonosian guard smiled and twirled his blaster. "Oh, plenty to do!" he said. "There's arena! Really cool!"

"What happens in the arena?"

"Kill things!" said the Geonosian.

Interesting, thought Boba. It was something to do. "Every day?" he asked eagerly.

"Oh, no," said the Geonosian. "Only special occasions."

*   *   *

Rules.

Rules are made to be broken.

That was *not* part of Jango Fett's code. *But it is part of the Kids' Code,* thought Boba. *Anyway, it oughta be.*

Boba was making excuses. He was getting ready to break his father's Off-Limits Rule.

He was preparing to slip out of the stalagmite city, to the red mesa.

He was trying to pretend it was all right, that it was something he had to do.

He was looking for adventure.

And he was about to find it.

The first part was easy.

The main door to the stalagmite city was on ground level, down below the landing pad. It was guarded by a drowsy Geonosian sentry, whose job was to watch for intruders, not escapees.

It was easy to slip past him.

As soon as he breathed the outside air, Boba realized how much he hated the musty smell of the stalagmite city. It was great to be outside!

He wanted to explore the glittering trails he had seen from above. He followed the first one he saw. It led down the side of the red rock mesa. The glitter was chips of mica — rock as smooth and shiny as glass that marked the trail and made it easy to follow.

Boba was just rounding a corner on a steep cliff when he heard a scream.

Then a growling noise.

He stopped — then proceeded more cautiously, step by step.

On the narrow trail ahead, two spike-backed beasts were fighting. They were growling, each pulling at one end of what looked like a furry rope.

The rope was hissing in a high-pitched tone.

The rope was a ten-foot snake, covered with fur. Its mouth and eyes were in the center of its long, furry body.

The lizards, which Boba assumed were the dreaded massiffs, were about to tear it in half with their long, razor-sharp teeth.

Then they saw Boba — and dropped the snake.

Boba backed up one step.

The massiffs both moved forward one step. Growling.

Boba backed up another step. The cliff was to his right. To his left, and behind him — nothing but air.

The massiffs moved forward again. Two steps this time.

Snarling.

Boba kept his stare locked on the massiffs' red eyes. He felt that if he looked away for even an instant, they would charge.

They moved forward again, side by side.

Boba knelt down and, feeling with one hand, picked up a slice of mica. Without looking, he tested it with his fingers. It was as sharp as a knife.

Suddenly he jumped up and threw it, spinning, toward the massiff on the right.

YELP!

A hit! But the other massiff was in the air, leaping toward Boba. He heard a snarl, and felt hot breath on his face, and ducked his head, and . . .

OOWOOOO!

The massiff missed him and flew off the cliff, howling as it fell toward the jagged rocks below.

Boba straightened up.

The other massiff was bleeding over one red eye. It was backing up, slinking away. . . .

Then it turned and ran.

The snake lay on the trail, nursing its wounds.

Boba's heart was pounding.

Maybe breaking the rules is not such a good idea, he thought. He was lucky to be alive.

He considered turning back — but decided that would be pointless. He was already halfway around the mesa. So he stepped over the dazed snake and continued on the path.

He had seen the path from above. He knew it would lead back to the entrance. He would sneak back in, and his father would never know he had been outside.

Then he heard something behind him. Something on the path.

The wounded massiff?

Boba felt a sudden chill. He looked back over his shoulder. It was the snake.

It was slithering along after him.

Boba stopped.

The snake stopped.

Its mouth in the middle of its body was smiling — at least it seemed to be smiling. And it was singing, a sort of rushing sound, like water falling. It sounded strange out here in the desert. It reminded Boba of the rain on Kamino, or the waves.

"Go away," said Boba.

The snake kept singing. It slithered a little closer.

Boba backed up. "Go away!"

The snake slithered still closer. Boba picked up a rock — a sharp piece of mica.

"Go away."

The snake looked sad. It stopped singing. It slithered away into the rocks.

Boba was making his way up the path, toward the top of the mesa, when he saw something strange.

There, on a flat ledge under a cliff on the side of the mesa, was a small ship. A starship.

A Delta-7! Could it be . . . ?

Just then Boba heard someone — or something — behind him on the trail.

He ducked behind a rock just in time.

The man who hurried past him along the trail was as familiar as the starship. As familiar, and as unwelcome.

It was the Jedi who had pursued them through the asteroid rings. The Jedi the torpedo had blasted. Obi-Wan Kenobi. Back again!

Boba watched from behind his rock as the Jedi opened his starfighter's hatch and climbed into the cockpit. Boba thought he was about to take off, but he didn't bother to close the hatch.

Whatever the Jedi was up to, Boba knew it was no good. He had to stop him. But how?

From where he was hiding, Boba could see over the rim of the mesa, all the way to the entrance to the stalagmite city. There was the drowsy Geonosian sentry he had slipped past.

The Jedi's starship was hidden from the sentry — but Boba wasn't.

But how could Boba raise an alert?

Boba picked up the biggest piece of mica he could find and wiped it on his sleeve until it shined like glass. Then he used it to reflect the light from Geonosis's sun, which was just peeping over the rings. He tilted the mica slab back and forth until he could see a flash of light across the sentry's eyes.

Then he did it again. And again.

Had the sentry seen it?

He had! He was coming down the path, toward the mesa's edge. Boba couldn't risk being seen, so he left the trail and scrambled up a steep ledge to the top of the mesa. When he got to the top of the mesa, he saw the Geonosian guard at the edge of the cliff, looking down. Boba knew he had sighted the Jedi starfighter, because he was talking excitedly on his comm.

Success! Or so it seemed. Boba ran toward the base of the tower — then skidded to a stop.

The gate was closed. He was stuck outside. How could he get inside without being discovered?

Then he got lucky again. The gate suddenly swung open and out came a squad of droidekas. They were in such a hurry to capture the Jedi that they didn't notice Boba, flattened against the rock wall.

He was able to slip through the door just before it closed behind the droidekas.

Safe! Boba was just about to breathe a sigh of relief when he felt a strong metal gauntlet on his shoulder. It felt gentle, yet stern.

"Where you heading, son?" asked Jango Fett. "Where have you been?"

"Uh, outside. Sir."

"Come upstairs. We need to talk."

Boba followed his father up the stairs and into the apartment. There was nothing he could say. There was nothing he could do. He was found out, and he knew it.

He sat down on the couch and watched while his father took off his battle armor and laid it carefully on the floor.

"Another adventure?" Jango Fett asked with a slight smile as he brewed himself a cup of nasty Geonosian grub-tea.

"I'm really sorry," Boba said. "Really really sorry."

"Sorry for what?" his father asked.

"Disobeying you."

"And that's all?"

"I-I guess," Boba said.

"What about lying to me?"

"I didn't lie," said Boba. "I admitted I was outside."

His father's smile was gone. "Only because you were caught. If you hadn't been . . ."

"I guess I would have," said Boba. "I'm sorry for that, too."

"I accept your apology, then," said Jango. "As a punishment you are confined to quarters until I say otherwise."

"Yes, sir." Boba breathed a sigh of relief. Confined to quarters meant grounded; it meant he had to stay in the apartment. It wasn't as bad as he had expected.

"It would be worse," said Jango Fett, "except that I owe you one."

"You do?!"

"Sure. For our Jedi friend. The one who somehow managed to escape us in the asteroids. He's been captured now, thanks to you. You alerted the sentry, even though it meant you might get in trouble. You did the right thing."

"Yes, sir. Thank you, Dad. I am sorry I disobeyed you."

"I am, too, Boba," said Jango Fett with a smile. "But I'm proud, as well."

"You are?!"

"I would be worried if you didn't disobey me at least once in your life. It's part of growing up. Part of the process of gaining your independence."

Boba didn't know what to say. Did his father really believe he had only disobeyed him this one time?

So he tried to hide his smile, and didn't say anything.

CHAPTER ELEVEN

Confined to quarters.

It could have been worse. But it was still pretty bad. Boba's lonely life got lonelier now that he was stuck in the apartment.

Jango Fett was very busy, talking business with the Count and the Geonosian they called Archduke, among others. Boba knew better than to try to sneak out.

Confined to quarters.

Boba missed his library friend, Whrr.

He was trying to construct a model starfighter from bits of wire when the door suddenly opened.

There in his battle armor stood Jango Fett. "Come, son," was all he said.

That was all he *had* to say!

Boba scrambled to his feet and followed his father down the stairs. He was glad to get out of the apartment, for any reason. And he always felt proud, following his dad. He knew that anyone who saw them was thinking:

That's Jango Fett. And that's Boba, his kid. He'll be a bounty hunter, too, someday.

*   *   *

There was a hush in the dim underground halls. Boba could tell something important was happening. He wondered what it was.

He knew better than to ask. He was lucky enough just to be out of the apartment.

At the end of a long corridor, they encountered a milling crowd of Geonosians. Some had wings on their backs; others didn't. A uniformed sentry waved them through, to the head of the line, and into a huge room with tall ceilings. Though the room was filled with Geonosians, it was so big it seemed almost empty. Every footstep and every cough echoed.

The Archduke and some other officials were seated in a sort of high box at one end of the imposing room, with about a hundred Genosians looking on. Two people stood looking up at them. Something about the way they stood told Boba they were prisoners. But proud, rebellious prisoners.

Jango and Boba squeezed into a crowd of Geonosians at the side of the room.

Somebody banged on something and the room got quiet. Almost, anyway. Everybody turned to look at the prisoners. Boba had to stand on tiptoe to get a good view.

One prisoner was dressed like a Jedi. He was a lot younger than the Jedi called Obi-Wan.

Maybe he's an apprentice, Boba thought. Though why anybody would want to be a Jedi was beyond him.

The other prisoner was a woman. And not just any woman. She was the most beautiful woman Boba had ever seen. She had a kind, gentle face — the sort of face he had always imagined his mother might have had, if he'd had a mother.

"You have been charged and found guilty of espionage," said one of the Geonosians.

Another chimed in: "Do you have anything to say before your sentence is carried out?"

The woman spoke up proudly. "You are committing an act of war, Archduke. I hope you are prepared for the consequences."

The Archduke laughed. "We build weapons, Senator. That is our business. Of course we are prepared."

Senator. Boba was shocked. He pulled his father's arm. "What's a Senator doing here, as a prisoner?"

"Shhhhhh!" Jango hissed.

"Get on with it!" demanded another official, a Neimoidian with mottled green skin and bright red eyes. "Carry out the sentence. I want to see her suffer."

It was the *other* Jedi that Boba wanted to see suffer, not the wannabe — and certainly not the woman. The persistent Jedi. The one they had killed again and again. Jedi Obi-Wan Kenobi.

But where was he?

The Archduke answered Boba's question. "Your other Jedi friend is waiting for you, Senator. Take them to the arena."

The arena! Finally they were going to get to see some action. It was what Boba had been waiting for.

And yet, somehow, he dreaded it.

CHAPTER TWELVE

Like almost everything else on Geonosis, the arena was carved out of solid rock. Yet because it was open at the top, the arena was the brightest place in the entire underground city.

The seats were filled with excited Geonosians, all flapping their wings and screaming with excitement, even though nothing was happening yet.

Vendors in bright costumes worked their way through the stands, singing and whistling to advertise their trays of live insects and other Geonosian treats. Boba loved it, even though he wasn't tempted by the squirming tidbits. He could hardly believe his luck. He was out of the apartment, no longer confined to quarters. He was in the arena, about to see a show. Plus, he and his father had the best seats in the house.

They were sitting with the Archduke and the other officials. Jango Fett and Boba followed the Count into the official box. The crowd started cheering wildly, and, at first, Boba thought it might be for his father, or even for the Count.

Then he looked down toward the center of the arena and saw the entertainment.

The Jedi prisoners.

They were chained to three posts: the young Jedi to one; the Jedi called Obi-Wan to another; and the beautiful woman to the third.

A fat Geonosian official cleared his throat and stood up to make a speech.

"The felons before you have been convicted of espionage against the sovereign system of Geonosis. Their sentence of death is to be carried out in this public arena henceforth."

The crowd was cheering like crazy, and the fat Geonosian sat down, smiling, as if he thought the cheering were for him.

The littlest Geonosian official stood up and waved his stubby arms. "Let the executions begin!"

Boba had mixed feelings. He hated the older Jedi, Obi-Wan, who had gotten lucky and humiliated Jango Fett by escaping twice.

Boba wanted to watch him die.

The apprentice Jedi, he didn't care about one way or the other. The problem was the woman. Boba didn't want to watch her die. Not at all.

One of the Neimoidians did, though. He was rubbing his chubby hands together so hard that they were starting to get red.

Boba looked away, disgusted. *It's guys like him who give executions a bad name,* he thought.

*   *   *

The crowd suddenly roared even louder.

And no wonder! Three barred gates down in the arena were opening. Riders in fancy costumes, mounted on orrays, were poking at monsters with sticks and spears, driving them into the central ring.

And what monsters! Boba recognized them all from books.

The first was a reek, a sort of killer steed with razor-sharp horns.

The second one was a golden-maned nexu with claws and sharp fangs.

And the third was an acklay, a monster with large, clenching claws, big enough to cut an orray in half with one pinch.

The crowd loved it, and why not? This was what the execution arena was all about. Death for fun.

Boba was even starting to get into it, a little bit.

The prisoners weren't, though. The woman had gotten out of her chains somehow and climbed to the top of her post.

Go! Boba thought. Even though he knew it was wrong, he hoped she would escape. He even had a fantasy that he would help her. Then she would join him to enjoy watching the two Jedi get killed.

Of course, Boba knew such a fantasy was

ridiculous. No one would escape. What was happening down in the arena was an entertainment, but it was also an execution.

The reek was running around the arena, slashing at the air with its horn and, it seemed to Boba, enjoying the wild cheers of the crowd. Then the great beast got serious. It charged the young Jedi's post.

WHAM! The reek hit the post a smashing blow, while the Jedi dodged sideways as far as his chain would let him. Then the Jedi jumped up, chain and all, onto the reek's back, which was, for him at least, the safest spot in the whole arena.

Cool move! Boba thought, in spite of himself.

Then the young Jedi did something even cooler. He wrapped the chain around the reek's horn, so that when the beast backed up and shook its head, the chain was torn free from the post.

Now the Jedi had a chain he could swing like a whip.

Boba cheered. Like the rest of the crowd, he was cheering for the reek.

The other Jedi, Obi-Wan, shifted deftly as the monster knocked the post flat, snapping it in two — and breaking the chain at the same time.

The nexu was after the woman. Its long fangs were bared, and it was trying to claw its way to the top of the post where she was perched, barely holding on.

Boba closed his eyes.

This one he did *not* want to watch.

The crowd groaned. AAAAAWWWWWW!

Boba opened his eyes. The Jedi Obi-Wan had grabbed a spear somewhere. He was using it to pole-vault over one of the orray riders. The acklay chasing him rammed into the rider and his orray, knocking them both flat. The acklay opened its huge claw, and then —

CRRRRRRUNCH!

It was the rider, an employee of the arena, who had been pinched in half. But the crowd of Geonosians didn't care. They just wanted to see blood. They didn't care whose blood it was.

Meanwhile, the young apprentice Jedi was riding the reek. He was using the chain for a bridle, controlling the beast.

The woman was still trying to get away from the nexu, which had ripped her shirt. Using her chain like a swing, she flew through the air, kicking the nexu into the sand and injuring its leg. Then she landed back on top of the post, out of reach.

Go! Boba thought again. Only to himself, of course.

The apprentice Jedi rode up on the reek, the beast completely under his control. The woman jumped on behind him. The nexu spat and snarled with rage — and then was attacked and killed by the reek. The Jedi called Obi-Wan jumped up behind the woman, so there were three of them on the reek, charging around the arena.

The crowd went wild. They weren't exactly cheering the gang of criminals — but they loved the excitement.

Boba cheered, too. He was glad to see the woman get away. So far, anyway.

It was all too much for the Neimoidian, though. He turned to Jango Fett. His beady little eyes were filled with rage.

"This isn't how it is supposed to be. Jango, finish her off!"

Boba watched, wondering what his dad would do. Jango didn't move.

The Neimoidian stared.

Jango Fett stared back.

The Count broke the silence.

"Patience, Viceroy," he said. "She will die."

A cheer went up and Boba looked down toward the arena.

The gates were opening again, all four of them this time. Droidekas rolled in, unfolding as they surrounded the prisoners, their blades gleaming wickedly in the light from the hole above the arena.

Before Boba could even blink, the droidekas had completely surrounded the three prisoners on their reek.

It was over.

Boba closed his eyes. He didn't want to watch. Then he heard a noise behind him.

A very slight clicking sound. He opened his eyes and turned, and saw a terrible sight.

A Jedi, standing behind his father.

The Jedi's face was dark, like fine wood. His eyes were narrow and cruel. His purple lightsaber was drawn, and ignited.

And held across Jango Fett's neck.

CHAPTER THIRTEEN

The Geonosians stopped cheering. The droid-ekas stopped advancing.

The reek, with the two Jedi and the beautiful woman on its back, stopped prancing and bucking and rearing. A hush fell over the entire arena and all eyes turned away from the Jedi and the droidekas. All of a sudden the show was not in the ring, but in the stands.

Everyone was staring at the officials' box, where the Jedi held the lightsaber to Jango Fett's neck.

We are the show! Boba realized with horror.

Jango Fett stood perfectly still. His Mandalorian battle armor was useless against a Jedi lightsaber. One flick of the Jedi's wrist and he would be decapitated.

Boba was scared.

As usual, the Count kept calm. Boba had noticed that he liked to turn everything into a game, even a bad situation. Even an emergency.

The Count seemed to know the Jedi.

"Master Windu," he said, in a smooth, oily voice, "how pleasant of you to join us. You're just in time for the moment of truth. I would think these two new boys of yours could use a little more training."

"Sorry to disappoint you," said the Jedi. "This party's over."

The Jedi gave a little hand signal. It looked to Boba as if lights were coming on all over the arena.

Lightsabers.

There were at least a hundred of them — some in the corners down by the ring, others up high in the stands. They came on all at once.

And each was in the hands of a Jedi.

Where had they come from? How had they all gotten in?

Boba was amazed at how bad the Geonosians' security was. And he was beginning to understand his father's grudging respect for the Jedi. They had their ways.

The Count, as always, tried to seem unimpressed. That was his style in a crisis.

"Brave but foolish, my old Jedi friend," he said. "You're impossibly outnumbered."

"I don't think so," said the Jedi called Windu.

He scanned the crowd with his hooded eyes. "The Geonosians aren't warriors. One Jedi has to be worth a hundred Geonosians."

But the Count came right back at him. "It wasn't the Geonosians I was thinking about."

It was the Count's turn to give a hand signal, even slighter and more subtle than the one the Jedi had given. Boba heard a sound like a storm on Kamino — a low rumble. Suddenly all the doors in the arena opened and every aisle in the stands was filled with Battle Droids.

The Battle Droids ran down the aisles with their lasers flashing, firing at the Jedi and scorching whatever else was in their way.

Lasers flashed overhead, and Boba ducked. The Jedi called Windu had gone from offense to defense in an instant. He was deflecting the droids' lasers with his lightsaber; it was like fencing with the air.

That was all Jango Fett needed. He crouched and fired the flamethrower that was built into his battle armor.

WHOOOOOSH!

Windu was engulfed in a torrent of orange flame, and his robe caught fire. It flared behind him like the exhaust of a rocket as the Jedi jumped out of the stands into the ring.

Jango let him go. He turned and went into action with the Battle Droids and the Geonosian troops, toasting the Jedi with vicious laser fire.

The Jedi all began to clump in the center of the arena, back-to-back, around the reek with the apprentice Jedi, Obi-Wan, and the beautiful woman still on its back.

The fight was on!

The reek wanted no part of it. It leaped into the air, throwing the three off its back. Then it ran in wild circles, snarling and snorting, stomping and stamping, crushing droids, Geonosian troops, Jedi, and bystanders under its hooves.

"Go!" Boba shouted, out loud this time. It didn't matter which side he was on — it was exciting to watch. Blood and bodies were flying. And the only person down there in the ring that he liked, the pretty woman, was unhurt, at least so far.

She was standing in the middle of the ring with the Jedi. Somebody had tossed her a blaster rifle. She was pretty good with it, too, blasting droids and Geos on all sides.

Jango was standing right beside Boba, taking a heavy toll from the stands, firing with deadly accuracy into the Jedi. It was the first time Boba had ever been in such a big battle with his father.

And he loved it!

"Stay down, Boba!" Jango ordered, and Boba knew better than to disobey. But he was able to peek over the railing and see down into the ring.

In the middle of all the confusion, Boba saw the Jedi called Mace Windu, the one his dad had scorched. He was mowing down droids and Geonosian troops with his lightsaber, rallying the Jedi with his boldness.

The reek saw him, too. The big, horned beast singled him out and started chasing him around the arena. Boba had to laugh. The Jedi had gone from hound to hare in about one second.

Mace Windu tried to make a stand. He skidded to a stop and slashed out at the reek with his lightsaber. But the reek kept coming — and knocked the lightsaber out of his hand.

It went flying, and the Jedi took off running again.

Jango Fett put his big, gloved hand on his son's head and growled, "Stay here, Boba. I'll be back!"

That turned out to be the last thing he ever told his only son.

CHAPTER FOURTEEN

Jango Fett used the jet-pack on his Mandalorian battle armor to rocket down into the arena. He landed right in the middle of the fighting. The runaway reek, which made no distinction between friend and foe, tried to stomp him.

From the stands, Boba saw his father dodging and rolling, trying to get out of the way. He bit his tongue to keep from screaming out. Those hooves were as sharp as knives.

But Boba needn't have worried. His dad rolled free, jumped to his feet, and proceeded to kill the beast. A couple of blasts and the reek was no more.

Then Jango Fett and the Jedi Mace Windu faced off, one-on-one, while the fight raged all around them.

Boba stood on tiptoe, trying to see, and at the same time dodging the bolts that were filling the air like angry insects. Super Battle Droids, more powerful than the Battle Droids, were now dominating the battle.

The dust rose in a cloud. The arena was filled with screams and shouts, the clash of lightsabers and bolts of laser fire. Boba yelled "Dad!" as he tried to see.

And then he saw.

He saw.

He saw the Jedi's lightsaber swing in a deadly arc. He saw his father's empty helmet go flying. He saw his father's body drop to its knees, as if in prayer.

Boba watched in breathless horror as Jango Fett fell lifeless onto the bloody sand.

"No!" Boba cried. *No, it can't be!*

The concussion from a nearby blast of laser fire knocked Boba down. He stumbled to his feet, ears ringing, and saw that the arena below was littered with bodies and pieces of droids and droidekas.

The acklay and the reek both were dead. The Jedi were outnumbered but still fighting. And the beautiful woman was right in the middle of it all, blasting droids and Geonosians alike.

Boba couldn't see his father or the Jedi he had been fighting. Had he dreamed it all? The swing of the lightsaber, the helmet flying off; the warrior falling to his knees, then toppling over, like a tree.

A bad dream, Boba decided. *That was it!* His father was somewhere back up in the stands. Boba knew that he didn't like to fight alongside droids. Jango Fett scorned the droids because they had no imagination. *Imagination*, he often said, *is a warrior's most important weapon.*

A bad dream, Boba thought, pushing his way down the stairs, toward the arena.

Even without imagination, the Super Battle Droids were winning. They were programmed to win, or at least to never give up. And even with all their losses, they far outnumbered the Jedi.

The droids in the stands kept firing, and the droids in the arena kept advancing, and soon there were only twenty or so Jedi left.

They stood in a clump in the center of the arena, back-to-back, lightsabers and lasers drawn. Trapped!

The aisles were full, so Boba climbed down from seat to seat, toward the arena. The Geonosians were cheering as the droids moved in for the kill. Then the Count raised his hand.

"Master Windu!"

Silence.

Boba stopped. *What's this?* He watched as the Jedi his father had been fighting stepped forward, covered with dust and sweat.

"You have fought gallantly," said the Count. "Worthy of recognition in . . ."

Boba didn't wait to hear more. He knew it was all a lie. It had to be.

He continued to jump from seat to seat, down toward the ring, pushing and shoving his way through the crowd.

He couldn't think. He didn't *want* to think. He just wanted to get into the ring and find his father, Jango Fett, who would tell him: *Don't worry, Boba, it was all a dream. A bad, bad dream.*

"Now it is finished," said the Count. "Surrender, and your lives will be spared."

"We will not be hostages for you to barter with, Dooku."

"Then I'm sorry, old friend," said the Count. "You will have to be destroyed."

The Count nodded and the droids were just about to fire into the little clump of Jedi, ending the whole thing, when all of a sudden the woman looked up.

All around the arena, the Geonosians started looking up.

Boba stopped and looked up, too.

Gunships were descending from the sky.

One, two, three gunships . . . six altogether.

They landed around the Jedi survivors. Doors in the ships opened and troops poured out, running down the ramps, firing at the droids. Boba knew the troops well, although he was surprised to see them. The Jedi began backing into the ships, still blocking laser blasts with their lightsabers.

The battle was on again, but Boba hardly noticed. He was running again, jumping from seat to seat, down toward the arena, as the gunships took off, with the Jedi still running up the ramps. Some were barely hanging on by their fingertips as the ships rose.

They were getting away. Not only the beautiful woman, but the Jedi he and his father hated. The Obi-Wan Jedi; the apprentice Jedi; the dark-faced fighter called Mace Windu. They were all escaping!

Boba didn't care. All he cared about was finding his father. He ran down the last aisle, pushing his way through the stunned crowd.

He climbed over the wall and jumped into the arena.

"Dad! Dad! Where are you?!"

The dirt and sand under his feet were soaked with blood. Bodies lay in heaps on all sides.

A droid that had been blasted in half was thrashing around in a circle, kicking weapons, droid pieces, and bodies in every direction.

One piece rolled toward Boba, hit his foot, and stopped.

Boba looked down and saw — Jango Fett's battle helmet.

Dad! With its narrow eye-slits, it was as famil-iar as his father's face. More familiar, in fact.

It was bloody. It was empty. It was as blank and as final as the period at the end of a book.

Over. End of story.

As he fell on his knees and picked up his father's battle helmet, Boba knew that the nightmare he had seen from the stands had been no dream.

It was real. All of it.

CHAPTER FIFTEEN

No one notices a ten-year-old kid, especially in the midst of a battle.

Especially when he is wandering in a daze, stepping over bodies and trails of blood, oblivious to the laser bolts whining through the air near his head or spinning into the bloody sand at his feet.

Especially when he is ignoring the shouts of the living and the screams of the dying; ignoring even his own cries.

Boba was invisible.

He was invisible even to himself. He didn't know what he was thinking or what he was feeling or what he was doing. He was numb. It was like walking through somebody else's dream.

He carried his father's empty battle helmet cradled in both arms, while he stumbled around the arena in the remains of the battle; while the troops were fighting the last of the droids and the gunships were departing with the rescued Jedi; while the panicked Geonosians were evacuating the arena in a stampede.

He carried the broken piece of his father's armor through the broken pieces of his world.

Did he think he could put his father back together?

Did he think he could put his life back together?

Boba didn't think anything. He was numb.

It was all gone, all shattered.

It had all come to pieces. Pieces lay everywhere. Pieces of droids, body parts, the dead and the dying. Those who were still alive, and some of those who weren't, were firing their blasters wildly.

Boba walked past a spinning droid, its right leg shot off. It was firing around and around as it spun, spraying the upper tiers of the arena and the panicked crowd of Geonosians.

Laser bolts hit the ground around him, throwing up geysers of sand. Boba didn't care. Boba walked on.

Crouching troops in battle armor hurried by, firing as they ran. One grabbed Boba's arm and threw him to the ground. "Get down!"

WHARROOOMM!

An explosion ripped through the air where Boba had been. He hit flat on his belly.

WHARROOOMM!

Another explosion — and Boba felt sand stinging his cheeks. He buried his face in his arms, next to the empty helmet. When he opened his eyes and looked up, he saw —

Dad! It was his father, Jango Fett, looking down at him! Boba reached up for his father's hand, and —

Then, suddenly, Boba saw how wrong he was. It was not his father. It was the trooper who had saved his life, or one of the others. For they all looked exactly alike beneath the armor. It was his twin, only older. It was his father, only younger.

It was one of the clones.

As he stumbled to his feet, Boba realized clearly — and with horror — that the troops that had poured out of the gunships were the clone army that his father had trained on Kamino. Here they were, in action for the first time, on Geonosis. And unbeatable, just as his father had predicted. But they were fighting on the wrong side. Fighting for the hated Jedi!

No! Boba thought, clenching his fists. His disappointment was replaced by feelings of betrayal and rage.

"Just a kid!" the trooper said. "Thought you were one of us." He ran with the other clones toward a departing gunship.

"I'm not one of you!" Boba muttered angrily. "And I never will be. I am Jango Fett's *real* son."

The arena was almost empty. The Archduke was nowhere to be seen. The Count was nowhere to be seen. The fighting was almost over. The last gunship was leaving, blasting upward through the opening over the arena.

Boba hardly noticed. He was looking down, not up. He didn't care about the clones anymore. He had a job to do. One last job for Jango Fett.

It was getting dark. The rings of Geonosis filled half the sky with an orange glow. With the helmet in his arms, Boba was walking in circles, stumbling through the blood-damp sand. Finally, he found what he was looking for. Stumbled across it, in fact.

It was his father's body, still clothed in the remaining pieces of Mandalorian battle armor, scuffed and bloodied.

Boba placed his father's helmet on his father's chest, then sat down beside him. He was tired and it was time to rest. He noticed a tear slowly making its way down through the gritty sand on his cheek. He wiped it away with his fist.

It was too soon to cry. Boba still had a job to do.

It was dark, or as dark as it gets on the ringed planet. The battle had moved out of the arena and had covered a wide part of the land.

The Geonosians — now under the control of the victorious Jedi — sent in squads of drones to pick up the dead. They were tossed on a fire. The smashed and broken droids were luckier. They were picked up by a scoop to be taken outside to a scrap pile, for recycling.

Boba was sitting by his father's body when the scoop rolled by, on its second pass through the bloody arena.

Boba knew what he had to do. He was not like the clones. He was Jango Fett's *real* son. It was his job to take care of his father's body. And as long as he did his job, he could put off feeling the feelings that he didn't want to feel.

The scoop whined and jerked as it moved from place to place, blindly scouring the sand for more parts. Boba dragged his father's body into the scoop's path, where it would be picked up. In his Mandalorian battle armor, Jango Fett felt to the scoop just like a droid. A broken droid.

Boba got on the scoop and sat beside his father. He held the battle helmet in his arms as the robot scoop headed out of the arena, down a long passage leading out to the desert.

Boba was doing his job. That was all that mattered.

For now.

The droid scrap yard was under the mesa where Boba had spotted the Jedi in his star-

fighter. It was an immense heap of broken cir-
cuits, busted arms and legs, wheels and heads
and steel knives and torsos.

The scoop made its dump and headed back
into the stalagmite city, through an underground
passage. Boba dragged his father's body off the
scrap pile and onto the rocky mesa.

The mesa seemed a better resting place. More
peaceful, and certainly more beautiful.

Boba removed his father's battle armor and
set it aside. He took one last look at the strong
arms and legs that had protected him. Then, using a broken droid arm for a shovel, Boba buried
his father in a sandy grave overlooking the desert.

The broken droid arm made a "J," and Boba
found another that he bent to make an "F." He
arranged them on top of the grave.

JF. Jango Fett. Gone but not forgotten.

Boba suddenly felt very tired. He sat down beside his father's battle armor. He wished he had
something to eat.

He shivered. The wind off the desert was cold.

Boba leaned back against the helmet and
looked up at the great orange rings that encircled
the planet. It was if they were holding it in their
arms. It was a peaceful sight. . . .

Boba slept peacefully all that night. His dreams
(and he forgot them) were of the mother he had
never had, and the father he had been lucky
enough to have. He awoke in the morning, rested

and surprisingly comfortable. Then he saw that a furry sand snake had wrapped itself around him as he slept, keeping him warm.

Startled, Boba jumped to his feet. The sand snake yelped in alarm and slithered away in a panic.

The same one? Boba wondered.

It didn't matter. What mattered was that his job was done, for now. His father was buried. The little grave with the *JF* on it was proof of that.

Looking at it, Boba realized how much he was going to miss the father who had protected him, guided him, watched over him — and loved him. Now he was alone, all alone.

And for the first time, and for a long time, he wept.

CHAPTER SIXTEEN

It was time to think clearly, time to make plans. Time to swing into action.

First things first, Jango Fett always said.

First was taking care of the Mandalorian battle armor: the suit, the helmet, the jet-pack, and all the weaponry. *It will be yours someday*, his father had said.

But for now, Boba was too small to wear it or even carry it around. So he cleaned it, then hid it in a small cave under a cliff. He would reclaim it later.

Second was the black book his father had left him; or rather, the message unit that was not-a-book.

It will tell you what you need to know.

Boba had to get back into the apartment to get it. That presented a problem, given the chaos created by the battle that had spread from the arena. He had been confined to quarters by his father, which meant that his retinal print might not open the door.

Boba got the battle helmet out of the cave to

bring with him, just in case. Since Jango almost always wore it, it would contain unlocking codes.

The next problem was getting into the stalagmite city. *I can do it,* he thought, hearing the crash of broken droid parts being dumped below the mesa.

First load of the morning.

So far so good, thought Boba as he rode the scoop through the underground passage. Dad would be proud.

He felt a sad thought approaching but he waved it away. There would be time for all that later. For now, the best way to honor his father was to learn and live by Jango Fett's code.

That would take some doing, but it would be worth it. It had been Jango's plan for his son. Now it was Boba's plan for himself.

Carrying the battle helmet, Boba ran up the long stairs toward the apartment. He passed only two or three Geonosians, and they hardly noticed him.

There are certain advantages to being ten. One is that no one ever thinks you are doing anything serious.

The door clicked open as soon as he touched it. The apartment was almost empty. Jango Fett had always traveled light. Boba looked for the black book in the box where he kept his few clothes and old toys.

It wasn't there.

Suddenly, he remembered his last trip to the library in Tipoca City. He realized, with horror, what he had done. He had gotten the black book mixed up with his library books. It looked just like a book, after all. He had returned it with them!

That's why Whrr had tried to call him back. But Boba had been in too much of a hurry to listen.

The information Boba needed was on Kamino!

Boba threw a few clothes and the battle helmet into his father's flight bag. Trying not to be noticed, he made his way along the vast halls of the stalagmite city, toward the landing pad where *Slave I* was parked.

He had learned that the best way not to be noticed was not to worry about being noticed. That was easy. He had something else to worry about.

Could he fly the ship alone, without his father watching over his shoulder?

There was only one way to find out.

Boba hurried on.

There was a guard at the door to the landing pad. Even though the Jedi had taken over the planet, the Geonosians were still guarding their property.

It was easy enough to slip past the guard while he was busy shooting the breeze with another Geonosian.

Or so Boba thought.

"Where are you going?" The guard blocked the door with his blaster.

"My dad," Boba said. He held up the flight bag. "He told me to put this into the ship for him."

"Which one?"

Boba pointed to *Slave I*. It was the smallest ship on the landing pad. Its scarred and pitted surface belied its great speed and maneuverability.

"Okay, okay," said the guard, turning back to his friend and his gossip. "But you only get five minutes. Then I'm running you off."

There was no time to check to see if *Slave I* was loaded and fueled. Jango had schooled Boba in all the flight checks, but he had also let him know that there are times when they had to be overlooked. Times when one had to trust to luck.

Boba hurried. The guard might come looking for him at any moment now.

Once he was in the cockpit, Boba pulled the helmet over his head and sat on the flight bag. To an outside observer, he looked like an adult. He hoped.

He kept his fingers crossed as he started the engines and engaged the drive, just as he had been taught.

So far so good. The guard at the door even

flipped him a lazy "good-bye" wave as Boba lifted *Slave I* off the platform and soared into the cloudless sky of Geonosis.

The ship felt familiar, almost like home. Boba was thankful for all the time he had spent practicing, and even pretending. Pretending is a kind of practicing.

The fuel was low, but sufficient to get him to Kamino. He was on his way. *Wish Dad were here to see me*, he thought. *I know he would be proud.*

That thought, instead of making Boba happy, brought a sudden sadness. He tried to shake it off.

He had other things to worry about.

Like the blip in his rear viewscreen.

It was a Jedi starfighter, on his tail.

The Jedi must have left him behind to watch for stragglers, Boba thought. *Is he here to follow me, to force me down, or to blast me out of the sky?*

Boba wasn't about to find out.

He knew he couldn't outrun the starfighter. And since he barely knew *Slave I*'s weaponry, he couldn't outfight him. That left only one option.

He had to outsmart him.

Instead of heading for space, Boba dove into the canyons and mesas that surrounded the stalagmite city. Using all the maneuverability of the craft, he sliced through the narrow canyons, turning right, then left, as fast as he could.

The starfighter was gaining. But that was okay. That was part of Boba's plan.

He remembered a trick his dad had told him about. A trick that had been used on Jango Fett once, and once only. (No trick ever worked on Jango Fett twice.)

Boba slowed where the canyon forked, left and right. He fired a missile at the canyon wall on the right, then turned left and landed on a narrow ledge under the shelter of a cliff.

Boba shut off his engines and waited. And waited.

If the trick worked the Jedi starfighter would see the marks of the explosion of the wall, and turn back. If it didn't . . .

If it didn't, the starfighter would appear around the corner, lasers blazing. Or call for backup, and the sky would fill with starfighters. Or . . .

Finally, Boba quit waiting and restarted his engines. The trick had worked. The Jedi starfighter had seen the explosion and turned back.

Boba grinned with satisfaction as he took off again. *He thought I hit the wall!*

Boba pushed *Slave I* up into the rings and beyond. He had never been alone in space before.

He had felt alone on the planet after his father's death, and particularly after burying him. But this was different. There is alone and there is *alone*.

There is no place more lonely than the vacuum of space. Because space is No Place.

In space, there is only Not. Zero. Absence. And the absence of absence . . .

Welcome to The Big Isn't.

Boba shivered at the thought of the emptiness around him—then pushed the thought aside. He had no time for The Big Isn't. He thought of his father and his code: *A bounty hunter never gets distracted by the big picture. He knows it's the little things that count.*

Boba had a job to do. He had to find the black book.

Boba slipped into high orbit, above the rings.

Geonosis below looked almost peaceful. It was hard to believe it had just seen the fierce fighting that had killed his father — and hundreds, perhaps thousands, of others.

It was a beautiful sight, but Boba didn't intend to spend time enjoying the view. He was already preparing the ship for a hyperspace jump.

For a return, this was a simple process. Since Kamino was the last place *Slave I* had been, all

Boba had to do was reverse the coordinates on the navcomputer.

The ship would take care of the rest.

So he did.

And so did it.

CHAPTER SEVENTEEN

In hyperspace, all sectors of the galaxy are connected. Near is far and far is near.

The ship was falling into a hole. No, out of a hole.

Boba was back in "normal" space.

He was floating in orbit around what looked like a ball of clouds stitched together with lightning.

Stormy Kamino!

Home. Or as much of a home as Boba Fett had ever known.

Boba rubbed his eyes, stretched, and put *Slave I* into descent trajectory. Gray clouds whipped past like torn flags. Lightning flashed on all sides; thunder boomed. As the little starship slowed below supersonic speed, rain splattered the cockpit's transparisteel.

Boba adjusted his speed and circled down slowly toward the lights of Tipoca City. He had watched his father do it several times, but this was his first time at the controls.

The funny thing was, he didn't feel alone. It was almost as if Jango Fett were right there behind him. Boba could almost feel the big hand on his shoulder.

Smooth! He cut the engines and eased onto the landing pad with hardly a bump.

The weather in Tipoca City was normal, which meant there was a big storm in progress — which was all right with Boba. He didn't want to be noticed.

He had worn the battle helmet, so that anyone watching *Slave I* landing would think there was an adult at the controls. But he needn't have bothered.

The landing pad was deserted. There was no one around.

Boba threw on a poncho and scrambled out of the cockpit, after setting the ship's environmentals on INPUT to take on air and water, both plentiful on Kamino.

Especially water — it was pouring rain!

The little library at the end of the street corridor was dark. Boba banged on the door.

"Whrr, are you there?"

Was he too late? Or too early? Boba was warp-lagged from hyperspace, and he realized he had no idea what time it was in Tipoca City.

"Whrr, please. Open up!"

The light behind the slot came on.

Boba wished the door would open so that he could go in, out of the rain, but the library was only a branch.

An awning slid out, though, to protect him from the rain. And he heard the familiar whirring and clicking inside.

"Whrr, it's me."

"Boba? You're back! Where have you been? What happened?"

A short question with a long answer. Boba told Whrr the whole story, from the time he and his father had left the planet in a hurry, to the horrible scene in the arena, where he had seen his father killed.

"Oh, Boba, that's terrible. You are an orphan, at only ten. Do you have enough to eat? Do you have any money?"

"Not exactly," said Boba. "A few crackers. An extra pair of socks."

"Hmmmmmm," whirred Whrr.

"I'll be okay," said Boba. "But I have to get something my father left with me. By accident I left it with you."

"A book?"

"Yes! You remember! It looks like a book, any-way. It's black, with nothing on the cover. I returned it by mistake, with the last books I brought back right before I left."

"I will be right back."

There was a whir and a click, a clank and a clatter. Soon Whrr was back — with good news!

"Here you are," he said, passing the black book through the slot. "But there is a fine, you know."

"A what!?"

"There's money due on this book. Quite a bit."

"It's not even really a book. Besides, I didn't check it out. It's *mine*! I left it with you."

"Exactly," said Whrr. "Which means the library owes you, let's see, two hundred and fifty credits."

"That's impossible —" Boba began.

"Sorry," said Whrr, passing the money through the slot. "A fine is a fine and must be paid. Now go on about your business, Boba, and good luck. Come and see me sometime. If you're ever around."

I get it, Boba thought. *I'm a little slow, but I get it.*

"Thank you, my friend," he said. "Someday I will come back to Kamino. I'll come by and see you then, I promise."

"Good-bye, Boba," Whrr said through the slot. The light went off and Boba heard a strange snuffling sound.

Must be the rain, he thought, *because everybody knows that droids don't cry.*

*　　*　　*

Boba could hardly believe his luck! Two hundred and fifty credits would buy groceries and supplies, even clothing, with some left over for fuel. This was vital — since he didn't know how to access his father's accounts.

And he had the black book! He patted it under his poncho, where he was carrying it out of the rain.

Before heading off-planet, Boba wanted to make one stop.

He wanted one last look at the apartment where he and his father had lived, where he had spent the first ten years of his life (although, of course, he didn't remember most of it).

Fortunately, it was on the way back to the landing pad.

As Boba rode up in the turbolift, he wondered about the locks. Had they been changed? Would they still recognize his finger and retinal prints?

He never found out. The door was wide open.

The apartment was dark. It was spooky. It no longer felt like home at all.

Boba closed the door and was just about to turn on the lights when he heard a voice behind him.

"Jango."

It was Taun We.

Boba could barely see her in the dim light from

the window. She was sitting on the floor with her long legs folded up out of sight under her long body.

"I saw *Slave I* come in," she said.

Boba crossed the room and stood in front of her.

Taun We looked up, startled. "Boba!? Is that you? Where's your father?"

Boba had always regarded Taun We as a friend. So he sat down and told her.

"You poor child," she said, but her words were cold and mechanical. Boba realized she wasn't such a friend after all.

"What were you about to tell my father?" he asked.

"The Jedi," she said. "They came and took the clone army, after you and your father left. They also wanted to question Jango Fett further. Now that he is dead, they will want you."

"My father hated the Jedi."

"I have no feelings for the Jedi," said Taun We. "Of course, we Kaminoans have few feelings for anything. It is not in our nature. But fairness requires that I tell you that they are after you. Just as I have told them that *Slave I* has landed in Tipoca City, and that you and your father would probably be coming here."

"You did *what*!?"

"I must be fair to all," said Taun We. "It is in my nature."

"Thanks a lot!" Boba said, heading for the door. He didn't bother to shut it after him. He couldn't believe Taun We had betrayed him to the Jedi. And he had thought she was a friend. Then he remembered his father's code: *No friends, no enemies. Only allies and adversaries.*

But what about Whrr? he thought as he pressed the button for the turbolift. *Wasn't Whrr a friend?* It was all too confusing to think about!

Boba was still lost in thought when the turbolift arrived. Then the door slid open, and —

It was a Jedi. A woman, young and tall.

Boba ducked aside and let her walk past. He kept calm, kept walking.

"Siri? You're too late," said Taun We from inside the apartment.

"You bet I'm gone!" said Boba as he opened the garbage chute and dove in. He closed his eyes and held his breath as he fell — down, down, down. . . .

It wasn't the fall he feared, it was the landing. The trash pile at the bottom would either be hard or . . .

OOOMPH!

Soft! Luckily, it was all old clothes and paper.

Boba was surprised to find himself grinning as he brushed himself off and ran out the door, toward the safety of *Slave I* — and flight!

CHAPTER EIGHTEEN

One good thing about stormy Kamino — there are lots of electrical disturbances to cover your tracks, even from radar.

Boba Fett knew that once he had lifted off the landing pad, he would be hard to follow. He buried *Slave I* in the thick, gray clouds, changed course a few times just to be sure, then punched up through the atmosphere into the quiet of space, and a long, slow orbit.

Back into The Big Isn't.

At last it was time to check the black book. The message that his father had promised would guide him after he was gone.

He grasped the cover tightly, prepared to pull hard. But the cover opened easily. Instead of pages and print, Boba saw a screen.

It was just as Jango had said. It was not a book at all, but a message screen. An image was coming into focus, a planet . . .

No, a face. Becoming clearer.

Boba's father's face.

It was dim but it was him. Jango Fett's eyes

were wide open. He looked sad, though; sadder than ever.

"Boba."

"Father!"

"Listen up, Boba. You are only seeing this because I am gone. Because you are on your own. Alone."

Boba didn't have to be told that. He was feeling very alone.

"That is the way. All things must end. Even a parent's love, and I am even more than a parent to you. Remember me, and remember that I loved you."

"I will, Father," Boba whispered, even though he knew his father could not hear. "I will never forget you."

"There are three things you need, now that I am gone. I can only point you toward them. These three things you must seek and find on your own."

On your own. The words had a cold, familiar sound.

"The first is self-sufficiency. For this you must find Tyranus to access the credits I've put aside for you. The second is knowledge. For knowledge you must find Jabba. He will not give it; you must take it. The third and the most important is power. You will find it all around you, in many forms. But beware, sometimes it is dangerous. And one last thing, Boba . . ."

"Yes, Father! Anything!"

"Hold onto the book. Keep it close to you. Open it when you need it. It will guide you when you read it. It is not a story but a Way. Follow this Way and you will be a great bounty hunter some-day. I was sure of it when I was alive, and I am sure of it still. . . ."

The picture was fading. "Father!"

The screen was blank. Jango Fett was gone.

Boba closed the black book. The cover sealed with a soft click.

Wow.

Boba didn't know whether to smile or cry, so he did both, while he sat with the black book on his lap. It was just a message screen, just a recording. But to him it was something very precious. It was his only connection with his father.

It was home and family.

He felt less alone.

Boba gave the black book a little pat and slipped it into the flight bag for later.

Then he stretched, and looked around.

Slave I was in high orbit. The planet Kamino was covered with storms far below. It looked like a marble made of mud and snow. On all sides, above and below, the stars beckoned.

Boba scanned through *Slave I*'s energy and environmental systems. Enough for one more hyperspace jump. Then he would have to refuel and refit.

Boba leaned back and planned his next step.

First things first, Jango always said. And according to Jango, or Jango's memory, Boba's first task was to find Tyranus. The Count. The man for whom Jango had created the clone army.

Boba had seen him in person, for the first time, on Geonosis. But he was sure that Tyranus had fled in the chaos of the battle in the arena. He didn't seem like the sort who would submit to being captured by the Jedi.

Where would he have gone?

Boba closed his eyes and remembered his father's voice, talking to the Jedi in Tipoca City: "I was recruited by a man called Tyranus on one of the moons of Bogden. . . ."

The moons of Bogden. That was a start.

Boba did a search in the ship's database. Bogden was a swampy, uninhabited planet in a far sector, surrounded by "numerous tiny satellites."

The moons of Bogden . . .

Boba punched in the coordinates. Then he hit the hyperdrive switch, and hoped for the best.

The stars started to dance as hyperspace wrinkled around the starship. Boba leaned back and crossed his fingers for luck.

"Here goes, Dad," he breathed as he closed his eyes. "I'll do my best to make you proud of me."

CHAPTER NINETEEN

Even though Boba had looked up Bogden in the database, he wasn't prepared for what he found when *Slave I* came out of hyperspace. "Numerous satellites" indeed!

He was orbiting what looked like a handful of pebbles someone had tossed into the air.

Bogden was a small, gray planet, surrounded by a swarm of tiny moons. Boba counted nineteen before he quit. It was hard to keep them straight. They were all shapes and sizes. The smallest was barely big enough for a ship to land on, while the largest had room for mountains, a city or two, and even a dry sea.

Day and night were erratic on these tiny circling worlds. Some were in darkness, some in light. Several had atmospheres; most did not. Boba scanned them all, looking for a city with a spaceport; or at least a town with a spaceport; or at least a town.

Many of the moons seemed uninhabited. Boba rejected one pear-shaped lump that oozed volcanic fumes, and another that was covered from pole to pole with gravestones. He decided against one that was covered in ivy that looked carnivorous. He passed on one that was all ice and one that was all ash and smoldering embers.

Finally Boba located a moon that was roughly spherical, half in light and half in darkness. At least it looked occupied.

He aimed for the largest cluster of lights he could find. The atmosphere was thin and shallow, and soon *Slave I* was in an approach trajectory over what looked like a small city scattered through several rocky valleys.

The ID-scan gave the moon's name as Bogg 4.

Boba aimed for a wedge of lights that looked like a landing pad. He clicked *Slave I* out of auto and began to set her down.

Smoothly and easily, and then . . .

Whoa! Something was rocking the ship, almost like a windstorm.

Boba fought the controls, trying to slow the descent.

Later he remembered a joke that went, "It wasn't the fall that was bad. It was just the last centimeter."

So it was with Boba. He made a perfect landing except for the very last part.

CRUNCH!

Slave I was tipped over on its side. Boba tried to right it, but it wouldn't move. According to his damage control panel, he had bent one of the landing struts.

At least no one was watching. The landing pad seemed deserted. Boba got out of the cockpit to survey the damage.

He felt dizzy. It looked bad. Two struts were good but the third was bent almost double.

He had no idea how to fix it. He got the flight bag down from the cockpit and looked through it for a repair manual. But there was only the black book his father had left him.

Boba pulled the black book out of the flight bag. Maybe there would be something in it that he could use. If he ever needed it, it was now!

The book opened easily. On the screen inside were two lines, looking like something out of Jango Fett's code:

Never tell the whole truth in a trade.
A favor is an investment.

Darn! Nothing about landing gear, Boba thought, closing the book.

He was putting it back into the flight bag when he heard a high-pitched voice behind him: "Whose ship?"

Boba turned.

A small humanoid was approaching. He had beady eyes, a long snout, and narrow, hooved legs. Boba recognized him by his chin beard and purple turban as a H'drachi from the planet M'Haeli. But modified: His right arm had been replaced with a multipurpose tool extension.

He wore coveralls with words stitched over the pocket:

HONEST GJON
STARSHIP SERVICE
"we will warp you"

"My ship," Boba said. Then he remembered that he was just ten, and looked it. "I mean — it's my father's."

"And where mmight this father of yours be?" asked the H'drachi.

"Unavailable at the moment," said Boba. "But you can talk to me."

"Honest Gjon at your service," said the H'drachi. "This is mmy landing pad. Which mmeans you owe me a landing fee. And it looks like you mmay need repairs as well."

"Looks like it," Boba admitted. Still feeling dizzy, he checked in his pocket for the credits Whrr had given him. He had planned to spend them on food and fuel. But now . . .

"How much to fix a strut?" he asked.

"How mmuch you got?" asked Honest Gjon.

Boba was just about to say two hundred and fifty credits, when he remembered the black book:

Never tell the whole truth in a trade. "Two hundred credits," he said.

Honest Gjon smiled at him. "Mmy mmy, what a coincidence. That's exactly how mmuch it costs."

So maybe the book helps with repairs after all, Boba thought as he gave Honest Gjon two hundred credits. He still had fifty for himself.

Plus, as a courtesy, the H'drachi agreed to waive the landing fee.

Boba gave Honest Gjon the access codes to *Slave I* and headed toward the lights of the little town. As soon as he started walking, he understood why the landing had been so difficult. Something was shaking Bogg 4. He had hardly gone ten steps before he ended up in a ditch.

He scrambled to his feet — then fell to his knees again. He felt dizzier than ever. It was as if the ground were rocking under his feet — and yet everything looked stable.

The rocks stayed stationary. The ground didn't move.

Boba stood up again, carefully. He took a step, then another. So far so good. The dizziness came and went, and, finally, Boba realized what it was that felt so strange.

It was the gravity itself! It was strong one moment, weak the next; now tilting him forward, now back. It came and went in waves.

Boba started off again, uneasily, holding onto a stone wall that ran along the road. By the time he got to the edge of the town, he was walking in a more or less straight line.

Or so he thought.

"I see you're a newcomer," said a voice from behind him. "A newcomer, yes."

Boba turned and saw a skinny male in a long black coat. He looked almost human except that he had white feathers instead of hair on his head, and his long fingers were slightly webbed. His face had a pinched, worried look, as if it had been shrunk.

"I can tell by your walk," said the being in the long black coat. "By your walk, yes."

"So what?" Boba said. The dizziness was making him sick to his stomach, and he wasn't feeling too friendly. "And why does the gravity here come and go like the wind?"

"Why, you have it exactly," said the man, or whatever he was. "It's the moons crisscrossing, now cancelling one another, now doubling their pull. It makes walking hard. That's why we locals prefer to soar, yes."

Boba looked for wings under the long coat, but he didn't see any. "You are a native, then, of this world?"

"Bogg 4? No. Of all the moons, of all the moons, yes. Say, you're pretty good, kid. Pretty good, yes."

"Huh?"

"At the walking. You've almost got it down, yes."

*   *   *

They introduced themselves to each other and walked together into the town.

Aia (for that was his name) explained to Boba that the moons of Bogden were a kind of outlaw heaven, where no warrants were served and no questions were asked.

"What does that mean?" Boba asked.

"It means that no one wonders why a ten-year-old boy is wandering around on his own. No one, yes."

And it was true. Boba was even more invisible here on Bogg 4 than he had been on Kamino or Geonosis. The streets in the town were crowded with creatures from every corner of the galaxy, all walking with the same rolling gait, and none paying the slightest attention to Boba and his companion.

The gravity came and went in waves as the moons overhead (and unseen "below") slid in and out and around one another, sometimes dark, sometimes bright. Boba was still dizzy. But he was getting used to it.

"So tell me," said Aia. "Why are you here, yes?"

"A short visit," said Boba cautiously. He wasn't sure who he could trust and who he couldn't. "I'm looking for a certain man who hired a certain bounty hunter."

"Lots of bounty hunters on Bogg 4," said Aia.

"Dangerous characters, yes. They come here to hang out and trade info. To get new jobs. They usually only associate with one another, yes. Never with their prey. You don't have a bounty on you, do you, yes?"

Boba laughed. "No way. I'm the son of a bounty hunter."

"Here, then," said Aia, stopping in front of a low tavern that fronted on the narrow street. A wooden sign said THE BONNY BOUNTY. "This is where the bounty hunters hang out, yes."

Boba looked in the window. The place was almost empty. He could see long tables, guttering candles, and a smoky fire. "I will wait here, then," said Boba, "while my ship is being repaired by Honest Gjon."

"Honest Gjon?" said Aia. "Oh dear, yes."

"Is something wrong?"

"I mean, no, nothing. Never mind. I'll leave you here, yes."

"You're not coming in?" Boba asked. Aia was his only guide. The last thing he wanted was to be alone in this strange place.

"No, my, uh . . . religion forbids it, yes."

"Religion, my reptilian foot!" Suddenly two figures were standing in the open door of the Bonny Bounty. "He's not coming in because he's a thief!" said one. "And he knows that we know it!" said the other.

On the right was a birdlike humanoid with

leathery skin and a broad beak. Boba recognized him as a Diollan. On the left was a green and reptilian Rodian. Boba knew that members of both species often became bounty hunters.

"This man is wanted for picking pockets!" the Diollan said.

"He stole from me, too," said the Rodian.

They grabbed Aia, each taking one of his skinny arms. "Oh, no, yes, no!" cried Aia, excitedly. He twisted and turned but couldn't get free.

Boba thought of the black book: *A favor is an investment*. Maybe if he did Aia a favor, it would pay off. At least he would have a guide. "How much does he owe you?"

"Twenty credits," said the Diollan. "Same here," said the Rodian.

"Here." Boba counted out forty credits, twenty for each. That left him ten. He wondered if it would be enough to buy something to eat.

The Rodian and the Diollan let go of Aia while they counted their money. As soon as his arms were free, Aia opened his black coat like a kite, bent his knees —

And jumped. Straight up. He soared up, over the rooftop, and out of sight.

Boba watched, dismayed. There went his investment.

The Rodian and the Diollan barely noticed. They turned and went back inside the tavern.

Boba followed them. Surely they owed him

something. He had done them a favor, after all, by giving them their money back. "Maybe you can help me," he said. "Are you bounty hunters?"

"Sure are," said the Rodian, with a laugh. "Are you bounty?"

"I am Jango Fett's son," said Boba. "Perhaps you knew him?"

The Diollan and the Rodian both looked at Boba with new interest. They took him to a table and signaled for the innkeeper, who brought food and tea. The tea was bitter but it made Boba feel less dizzy.

In fact, the more he drank the less dizzy he felt.

"We knew your father," the Rodian said.

"A great bounty hunter and a great man," said the Diollan.

Boba told them the whole story of how his father had died and everything that had happened since. He hoped he could trust them because they were his dad's colleagues.

Somehow, talking about his father's death made Boba feel better. It made it seem less like a tragedy and more like a story. Boba wondered if that was why people told stories — to get over them.

"My father mentioned a client," Boba said. "I thought I might find him here."

"His name?"

"Count, uh . . ." Boba suddenly remembered

that Tyranus was a name no one was supposed to know. "Count Dooku," he said, using the name the Count had used on Geonosis.

"Dooku?" said the Diollan.

"Not here!" said the Rodian.

"You must go to — Coruscant!" they both said together.

"Are you sure?" Boba asked, confused. Coruscant was the planet where the Republic and the Jedi had their headquarters. Why would Tyranus be there?

"Yes, yes, absolutely sure!" said the Rodian.

"Positively. Go to the Golden Cuff tavern in Lower Coruscant," said the Diollan.

"Tell the bartender who you are looking for," they both said together. "He'll know immediately what to do!"

"Thanks!" said Boba. He tried to pay his bill but the bounty hunters insisted on treating him. Boba thanked them again and headed back to the landing pad where he had left his starship with Honest Gjon.

As soon as he had left, the Diollan and the Rodian turned to each other and grinned.

"That's the best kind of bounty," said the one.

"The kind that delivers itself and saves us the fuel . . . *and* the trouble!" said the other.

* * *

The tea was wearing off, Boba could tell, as he headed back for Honest Gjon's landing pad. He felt dizzy again. Not as dizzy as before, but a little bit.

The moons of Bogden were wheeling across the sky. Some were small, some were large; some were dark, and some were bright.

Boba could hardly believe his luck. He had picked the right moon, Bogg 4. He had found the right bounty hunters, the Diollan and the Rodian. And on his very first try, he had located Tyranus. He had even eaten dinner, and it hadn't cost a credit!

A favor is an investment. He had meant to do the favor for Aia. Instead he had done it for the bounty hunters, and it had paid off.

Now all he had to do was get in his starship and go to Coruscant.

There was only one problem. The landing pad was empty.

Slave I was gone.

CHAPTER TWENTY

Boba sat down on the ground, under the wheeling, spinning Bogden moons. He was dizzy again. The tea had worn off completely.

His starship was gone. So was the black book that contained Jango Fett's code. So was his father's battle helmet — his legacy.

Even his money was gone, except for ten credits.

Gone, all gone. How could he have been such a fool? How could he have let his father's memory down? How could he have trusted Honest Gjon? He put his head in his hands and moaned in dismay and self-disgust.

Then he heard a clucking sound. "Tut, tut, yes."

It was Aia. "I was afraid of this," the skinny moon-being said. "That's why I ran back. But I was too late. That Honest Gjon is a crook, yes."

"So are you," Boba pointed out. "You steal things."

"Only my fingers steal," said Aia, holding up both webbed hands. "And only what I need, yes.

To prove it, I will help you find Honest Gjon. Not so honest, yes."

Boba felt a glimmer of hope. "Where did he go?"

"His shop. He tears ships down for parts. So they can't be traced, yes."

"Then we must hurry," said Boba, jumping to his feet. "Before he begins to tear *Slave I* apart. Where is this shop of his?"

Aia pointed straight up, toward a jagged, spinning moon.

"Oh, no!" Boba sat back down. "He has taken it to another world."

"Yes, of course. He thinks you can't follow, yes."

"But he's right! I can't!"

"But you can," said Aia. "Come. Come with me, yes." And he took Boba's hand and pulled him to his feet.

"If you were any older or any bigger, this would be a problem, yes," said Aia as he led Boba up the path. "As it is, we may just make it, yes."

"Make what?" The path twisted and turned up a rocky hill overlooking the landing pad.

"You will see, yes."

Boba saw — and didn't like what he saw.

The path ended at a cliff.

Boba gripped Aia's big hand and leaned out, looked up, looked down. Above, he saw darkness, a few moons, and many stars. Below, he saw only darkness.

He was dizzy again.

"The gravity waves rise and fall with the moons, yes," said Aia. "If you get high enough, and if you know what you are doing, you can ride them. Like a bird on the wind, yes."

All of a sudden, Boba got it. And he didn't like it.

He backed away from the edge of the cliff, but not fast enough. Aia was already stepping off into thin air — and pulling Boba with him.

Boba was falling.

Then he wasn't.

He was rising, soaring, slowly at first and then faster, faster, faster. Rising up through the air.

"You have to ride the vectors, yes," said Aia, whose coat was spread wide like a kite, like wings. He squeezed Boba's hand. "When one vector gives out, we cross to another, yes."

Let's hope so, thought Boba.

Aia pulled Boba with him. They plummeted down, then started to rise again.

They were heavy one moment, weightless the next.

Boba ignored the lump rising in his throat for as long as he could.

Then he lost it.

"Yu-ck!" said Aia. "If I had known you were going to do that . . . I would have . . . yes . . ."

"Sorry," said Boba.

He was feeling less dizzy. The higher they soared, the easier it got. All Boba had to do was hang on to Aia's hand and follow. Other figures darted in and out of the clouds. All of them were small like Aia.

Aia waved at them.

"We are the couriers, yes," he said to Boba. "We are the only ones light enough to travel from world to world. You too, yes. As long as you stay with me."

Don't worry, Boba thought, squeezing Aia's hand. *I'm sticking with you!*

It was getting cold. Boba looked down. He immediately wished he hadn't.

Bogg 4 was a tiny lump of stone and dust, far away. The stars were too bright. It was hard to breathe.

We're almost in space! Boba thought. *We have soared too high!*

"There, Bogg 11, yes," said Aia, pointing up ahead to where a smaller, darker moon was about to cross Bogg 4's orbit. Gravity was pulling at both moons, tangling their clouds together in long streams, like seaweed.

"The foam is where the atmospheres brush

one another," Aia said. "That is where we make the jump, yes."

"And if we miss . . ."

"Space is cold," said Aia. "Eternity is cold. Hang on, hold your breath, yes!"

Boba held his breath. But he couldn't hold on.

His fingers were numb and stiff with cold. He felt Aia's hand slipping away.

"No!" cried Boba silently, since there was no air with which to shout or scream.

No air to breathe.

He closed his eyes. He was spinning, weightless, drifting away into The Big Isn't. The nothingness of space. Of death.

Here I come, Dad, he thought. It was almost a peaceful feeling. . . .

Then he felt gravity pulling at him like fingers, gently. Slowing his spin. Pulling him down.

Boba could hold his breath no longer. He gulped, expecting the cold rip of vacuum in his lungs.

Instead, he tasted air. It was hardly sweet but it tasted great to Boba.

He opened his eyes.

Aia had him by the hand again.

They were soaring in the sky of a different world. A smaller, smokier world.

"Bogg 11, yes," said Aia.

They circled down toward Bogg 11 in long

loops. Boba saw *Slave I* parked in a rocky little valley, surrounded by piles of spaceship parts.

"Luckily he's just getting started," Aia said. "We made it, yes."

They landed on the side of a small, steep hill. Boba fell and rolled to a stop. He got up, dusted himself off, and started running down a rocky path, toward *Slave I*.

Honest Gjon saw them coming and stared.

"What if he won't give it back?" Boba asked. He picked up a rock. He wished he had a blaster.

"Don't be silly," said Aia. "Put down the rock. Thieves have honor, yes?"

Yes. It seemed so. Sort of, anyway.

"Can't blame a guy for trying!" said Honest Gjon, throwing up his hands. The bearded H'drachi's smile seemed genuine.

Boba shook his head in exasperation and looked into the cockpit. The flight bag was still there. The battle helmet and the black book were inside it. Maybe there was honor among thieves after all.

Boba tried the book, and it opened.

Money is power.

* * *

Not much help, Boba thought, *since I don't have any.* He closed the book and put it back into the flight bag.

Honest Gjon was watching Boba's every move. "What does it say?"

"It says you're supposed to give me my money back."

"No way!" said Honest Gjon. "I fixed your strut, didn't I?"

"He did, yes," said Aia.

"Can't blame a guy for trying," said Boba.

They all shared a laugh.

But while Boba laughed, he tried to think of his next move.

CHAPTER TWENTY-ONE

Boba found that he liked these outlaws of the moons of Bogden. Crime was just a game to them. They were like bounty hunters, in a way.

"Coruscant's a dangerous place," said Honest Gjon, when Boba told him where he was going.

"And expensive," said Aia. "You have no money, yes?"

"I have ten credits," said Boba. "I guess that'll have to be enough."

"There are ways to get money, yes," said Aia.

"Such as?"

"Such as crime," said Honest Gjon. "I happen to know of some mmoney being smuggled from Bogg 2 to Bogg 9. A few fellows with a good ship and a little luck could take what they needed."

"You could be one of those fellows, yes," said Aia.

Boba was intrigued. *Money is power.* "You're talking about a hijacking? A robbery?"

"An interception," said Honest Gjon. "Not exactly a robbery, since it isn't real mmoney, yes. It's counterfeit credits. They are made on Bogg 2, then sent by light-air balloons to Bogg 9 when the alignment of the mmoons is just right."

"The atmospheres brush together and the balloons pass from world to world," said Aia. "Like we did, yes."

"A smugglers' trick," said Honest Gjon. "And if we pick off one balloon on the way, no one will mmiss it."

"They will think one just got away, yes," said Aia. "Of course, catching it on the fly requires a *very* good pilot with a *very* good ship. You may be too young, yes."

"I want a third," said Boba. "When do we go?"

"In about ten minutes," said Aia. He looked at Honest Gjon and winked. "I told you he would do it, yes?"

From space, Bogg 2 looked like a dry dirt clod, spiked with mountains. Boba cruised over slowly, then put *Slave I* into a slow holding orbit just above the atmosphere.

"No lights, no electrics, no radio," said Honest Gjon. "That way we can't be seen. The trick is to try to catch the balloon as it rises. If you get close, I will hook it into the hatch."

"We should let the first one go, so they don't suspect anything, yes," said Aia. "Then grab the next one."

"Sounds like a plan," said Boba.

"Look," said Honest Gjon. "Here comes number one."

He handed Boba a viewfinder. Boba saw a red balloon rising out of a mountain valley.

He handed the viewfinder to Aia. The balloon rose swiftly in the low gravity. It streaked past, into the stormy space between the moons. A gondola hung below it, packed with bales of credits.

Money! thought Boba with a grin. *Money is power!* If only his father could see him now. He knew he would be proud.

"Here it comes," said Honest Gjon. The second balloon was on its way. It had an even larger gondola hanging beneath it. *Even more money*, Boba thought.

Aia tracked it with the viewfinder and then with his naked eye, while Boba operated the ship. "Back up a hair, yes. Now forward. Now up, yes. Whoa!"

Honest Gjon opened the ramp and pulled in the balloon. "Got it!"

"Great," said Boba. "Now let's close the ramp and get out of here."

"One more," said Aia.

"I thought two was the plan," said Boba. "They will see us if we stay too long. They'll send someone up after us."

"One mmore can't hurt," said Honest Gjon. He held up a fistful of brand-new credit notes.

Why not? thought Boba. *More is better.* If the black book didn't say that, well, it should!

He pulled the ship back into place and held it steady, adjusting for the varying gravity of the spinning moons.

"Number three!" said Aia. Honest Gjon went to open the ramp.

The red balloon was getting closer and closer. Honest Gjon went down to open the ramp and pull it in. The gondola underneath it was even bigger than the one before.

More money! *More is better,* Boba thought, with a grin.

"Ooooops," said Honest Gjon. "Slight problem."

"You're all under arrest for counterfeiting," said a gruff voice.

Boba turned and saw Honest Gjon in the doorway. He was not alone. Standing beside him was a trooper in a security uniform, holding a blaster.

Oh, no! thought Boba.

"It's not our money," said Aia. "It's all a mistake, yes. We'll give it back!"

"Who cares about the money?" said the trooper, with a cruel smile that was all teeth. "I'm officially confiscating this ship in the name of the law. It's contraband."

Boba was thinking: *No way!* Give up *Slave I,* his father's ship? But what could he do with a blaster pointed at his face?

Then he remembered a trick Jango had taught him.

"Move over, kid," said the trooper. "And put your hands up where I can see them. Now!"

"Yes, sir." Boba set the power on FULL AHEAD and punched in DELAY 4. Then he stood up with his hands over his head and slowly backed away from the controls. He counted silently: four, three —

The trooper grinned. "That's better," he said, motioning with his blaster toward the open hatch. "Now grab some air, all three of you."

Two, one —

Boba lunged, grabbing the back of the pilot's seat as the engines roared to life and *Slave I* suddenly sprang forward. The trooper, Aia, and Honest Gjon all flew through the air and hit the back wall in a clump.

WHACK!

THUMP!

Boba held onto the seat and threw the ship into a sharp turn. Honest Gjon and Aia grabbed the dazed trooper, one on each arm. They dragged him to the still-open hatch — and shoved him out!

Boba grimaced as he brought the ship back under control. "Murder of a security trooper. Now we're in big trouble!"

"He's got a parachute, yes," said Aia.

"He's no trooper, anyway," said Honest Gjon. "That uniform was as counterfeit as the credits. That was a hijacking that failed."

*　　*　　*

"We did it!" said Boba as he set the ship down on Honest Gjon's landing pad. His heart was still pounding, but he had saved *Slave I*. And made some money, too.

"How many credits do we have?" he asked. "Let's divide them three ways, so I can get out of here."

"That's the bad news, yes," said Aia. "They all flew out the door when we shoved him out."

"All but one," said Honest Gjon. He handed Boba a hundred-credit note. "Take it, you deserve it all. And you're going to need it on Coruscant."

Boba put the money into his pocket with the pathetic little ten. Even though he had only made a hundred credits, he felt that Jango Fett would have been proud.

He had found out what he needed to know on the moons of Bogden. He had even made a few friends (or, as Jango would have called them, allies. *No friends, no enemies. Only allies and adversaries*).

Now it was time to head for Coruscant and find Tyranus.

He shook hands with Honest Gjon, but Aia insisted on giving him a big hug. "Boba, continue your quest, yes. But take care. You are too trusting. Watch your back, yes?"

"Yes," said Boba. "Thanks, Aia."

They hugged again, then Boba got into *Slave I*

and took off. It was only after he was in deep space, preparing to shift into hyperdrive, that he noticed that the hundred-credit note was missing from his pocket.

And so was the ten.

CHAPTER TWENTY-TWO

In the endless, intricate web of civilized and half-civilized worlds that make up the Galactic Core, some planets are obscure and hard to find. And others are hard to miss.

Coruscant is in the second category.

The coordinates are easy to remember and even easier to punch into a starship's navigational computer:

zero zero zero.

It is here that civilization begins. At the heart of the Core Worlds. At the very center of the Known Universe.

Coruscant. The planet that is a city; the city that is a planet.

Boba awoke when *Slave I* shuddered out of hyperdrive and slid into normal space.

He shook his head to clear it of the dreams that always crowded in during hyperspace jumps.

And there it was. The legendary city planet, covered by pavements and roofs, towers and balconies, parks and artificial seas. Coruscant was one immense metropolis from pole to pole.

Not a green spot nor an open field; no wilderness, no forests, no ice caps. Coruscant was one enormous planetwide city, covered by slums and palaces, parks and plazas. It spun below in all its glory, welcoming *Slave I* as it had welcomed pilgrim and pirate, politician and petitioner, wanderer and wayfarer since the Republic's first beginnings millennia ago.

And now it awaited Boba Fett. An orphan seeking only to please his father's ghost.

Hopeful again at last, Boba eased *Slave I* into suborbital approach, past the big orbiting mirrors that gathered and focused the light of Coruscant's faraway sun.

The starship hit the atmosphere and began to slow. Boba descended in big looping turns, past the towers of the wealthy and powerful, past the hanging gardens, and into the commercial zones reserved for uninvited visitors. With traffic crowding in on all sides, this was a much more harrowing approach than on Kamino or the moons of Bogden. Boba's heart tightened in his chest. Would they find him here?

He felt a slight bump and let go of *Slave I*'s controls. The ship was locked into autopilot, being flown "by wire" on a microbeam. It would land itself.

That was fine with Boba. He had other things to worry about. Money, for starters. He would need to pay his landing fees before he could take off again. Then there was the problem of the Jedi. If they were really after him, as Taun We had warned, they might have a warrant out on *Slave I*. He could be arrested as soon as he touched down.

He needed some guidance. Maybe the book would help. It seemed to open when he needed it, or at least when it had something to say.

He pulled it out of the flight bag. Sure enough, it opened. But the message was even more mysterious than usual:

Watch out for things that go too well.

That's hardly my problem! Boba thought. He closed the book, disgusted, and put it away. He watched nervously as the ship eased in toward the spaceport, slipping smoothly between the towers and under the lighted walkways and gardens of Coruscant.

Slave I bumped down, light and easy. No alarms went off.

Boba lowered the ramp. He scanned the landing pad, ready to run if need be.

Nobody was watching. Nobody was around.

This was Coruscant. Nobody cared about an insignificant little ship like *Slave I*. Or its insignificant little ten-year-old pilot.

Boba's first emotion on landing was relief.

His second was fear. The Jedi had eyes and ears everywhere. And especially on Coruscant. Would they find Boba before he found Tyranus?

Boba didn't fear the Jedi as much as he feared failure. Would he disgrace his father's memory by failing in his first test, the search for Tyranus — and self-sufficiency?

"Welcome to Coruscant," said a disembodied droid voice.

"Sure, whatever," muttered Boba.

Carrying his flight bag with the black book and the battle helmet, plus a few extra pairs of underwear and socks, he climbed down out of the ship. He started down the escalator toward the streets.

Boba had read enough about Coruscant to know that it was arranged in layers according to class and function.

The upper levels were for the rich and powerful. Looking up, Boba could see their towers and gardens reaching up into the clouds.

The middle levels, where he had landed, were for both business and pleasure. The streets were filled with creatures from all over the galaxy, rushing around, buying and selling, or just sightseeing.

The lower levels were said to be dangerous. They were the outlaw zones, filled with fugitives, pirates, and criminals — all the denizens of the underworld that lay beneath the Imperium.

Boba hoped all would go well on the lower levels when he went to find the Golden Cuff. He'd had quite enough adventure, thank you. He just wanted to find Tyranus.

Boba was in luck.

The Golden Cuff was a little hole-in-the-wall on the upper layer of the lower levels, just under the lower layer of the middle levels.

It was far enough down that the light was dim and the neon signs could glow all day. But not so far down that one had to hire a posse of armed guards to cross the street.

Boba walked in through the sliding door.

The bar was deserted except for the bartender, a four-armed being who was using two of his arms to wash glasses, one to count credits, and one to wipe the bar with a wet rag. His skin was a dark crimson, and a proprietor sign named him as Nan Mercador.

Boba put his flight bag on the floor and sat on a bar stool.

"No kids allowed!" said Mercador, wringing out the rag and tossing it onto the bar. "And that means you!"

"I'm not a customer," said Boba. "I'm not looking for a drink. I'm looking for a — uh, relative. Named Dooku."

The bartender's face brightened. "Dooku!" He looked at Boba with new interest. "Dooku. Oh, yes, of course. Absolutely. He's a good friend of mine. Let me give him a call."

Mercador started punching numbers into a comm unit. "Dooku? Is that you?" he said. "Somebody here to see you." Static came up on the comm screen behind the bar, as if it were a long-distance planet-to-planet call. The bartender smiled at Boba. "How about a juice while you are waiting?"

"I don't exactly have any money," said Boba.

"It's okay," said the bartender, wiping the bar with one hand and filling a mug with two others. "It's on the house!"

The juice was cold and tasted great. Boba could hardly believe his luck. He had only been in Coruscant for an hour or so, and already he had met a friendly bartender who actually *knew* Tyranus (excuse me, Dooku!), and now he was drinking a free juice!

Suddenly he remembered the black book: *Watch out for things that go too well.* Could it be that —?

The static on the comm screen went away, and Boba saw two familiar faces. Neither was Tyranus. The one on the right was the Diollan; the one on the left was the Rodian. The two bounty hunters from the moons of Bogden.

"That's him!" said the Rodian. "Grab him! You can bring him to the Jedi for the reward." Boba tried to slide down off the stool and run. But it was too late. Strong hands grabbed his right arm.

And his left arm.

And his left leg.

And his right leg.

Nan Mercador came out from behind the bar and lifted him off the stool, into the air.

"Hey!" Boba yelled. "Let me go!"

"Not a chance," said the bartender, holding Boba over his head. "You're worth money!"

"This is a mistake!" Boba said.

"No mistake, kid," said the Rodian on the comm screen.

"You're bounty," added the Diollan.

"The Jedi know you're coming," said the Diollan to Mercador.

"They will give you your share in cash," said the Rodian.

"I should get half," said the bartender as he started toward the door holding Boba over his head with all four arms. "I saved you both the trouble of coming here."

"Too late for that," said the Rodian.

"It's already been arranged," said the Diollan as they hung up.

The screen went black.

Think fast, thought Boba, squirming and kicking helplessly near the ceiling. *And if that doesn't work, think faster!* He stopped squirming. "Don't be a fool," he said. "Count Dooku will pay twice as much as the Jedi. And you won't have to split it with anybody."

"I won't?" Nan Mercador stopped. But he didn't let go of Boba. "Are you sure?"

"Positive," said Boba. "Set me down, and I will call him myself. You can ask him."

"You must think I'm a dope," said Mercador, still holding Boba so high above his head that he almost scraped the ceiling. "Besides, you don't know his number. You asked me to find him, remember?"

"I was just testing you," said Boba, looking at the ceiling light near his left foot. It was only centimeters away. "But you don't have to believe me. You can call him yourself. The number is . . ."

He rattled off a string of numbers, hoping they would sound right. Apparently they did. The bartender let go of Boba's left foot and began punching them into the comm unit on the bar.

Boba was ready to move. As soon as his foot was free, he kicked the light as hard as he could.

CRASH! It shattered, showering glass down onto the bar, the stools, the floor. . . .

Mercador lifted his hands to protect his head

from the falling glass. Boba fell, straight down, headfirst. At the last moment he managed to twist in the air like a diver and land on his feet. He scrambled toward the door, which slid open —

And revealed two gleaming boots, blocking his way. Above them were two shapely legs. And above them —

It was a woman, holding a vicious-looking blaster. She grabbed Boba's arm with one hand. She raised the other hand and fired.

ZZZ-AAA-PPP!

The bartender howled with pain and sat down on the floor in the middle of the broken glass.

"It's set on stun," she said. "But one false move and it goes to kill."

"Cool," said Boba, looking up at his rescuer. She looked dangerous. That made her even more beautiful to him. "Who are you?" he asked.

"Aurra Sing," she said. "But never mind that. Let's get out of here."

Boba didn't have to be asked twice. He grabbed his flight bag and followed her out onto the street, toward a parked hovercraft that was idling quietly on the narrow street.

"Bounty hunters," he explained breathlessly. "They betrayed me. I never should have trusted them!"

"Bounty hunters can always be trusted," Aurra Sing said. "Trusted to do what they are paid to do." She opened the door of the hovercraft. "I know, because I am a bounty hunter myself. Get in, young Boba Fett."

"You know my name?"

"Of course. The bounty hunter always knows the bounty's name."

Boba backed up, ready to run.

"Get in!" Aurra Sing patted the blaster in the gleaming holster that matched her boots. "It's very painful, even set on stun. Don't make me try it on you."

Boba gave up and got in. He groaned as the hovercraft lifted off. He'd thought he had been rescued. Instead, he had been captured again!

As the hovercraft rose higher and higher, winding through the towers and hanging gardens of Coruscant, Boba sat back in his seat and sulked, disgusted with himself.

"Watch out when things go too well." I should have known better, he thought. *I will never trust anybody ever again!*

He was surprised when Aurra Sing landed the hovercraft at the spaceport, right next to *Slave I*.

"Aren't you taking me to the Jedi?" he asked. "I thought you were a bounty hunter."

"I am," she said. "But I would never work for the Jedi. My client lives on another planet altogether. That's why we are taking your ship. You can fly it, can't you?"

"What if I say no?"

She patted her blaster again.

Boba opened the ramp and checked out *Slave I*'s systems. To his surprise, Aurra Sing paid off the landing fees, and even tipped the droid.

"Low orbit first," she said. "Then hyperspace. And no funny business. I'm not known for my sense of humor."

"No kidding," Boba said under his breath. Then he asked, "Do you mind telling me who put out a bounty on me, and where we're going?"

"You'll find out the *who* soon enough," she said. "The *where* is an outer rim world called Raxus Prime."

"Excuse me? I must have heard you wrong. I thought you said Raxus Prime."

"You heard right."

"But — that's a seriously uninhabitable planet."

"I know. And we're late. So drop us into hyperspace, and let's go."

CHAPTER TWENTY-THREE

Boba had read about Raxus Prime, but he had never seen it, not even in pictures. Few had. Who would want to?

Raxus Prime was the most toxic planet in the galaxy. It was the dump for all the debris and detritus of a thousand civilizations.

It didn't look so bad from a distance. *Sort of like Kamino,* Boba thought, as he dropped out of hyperspace, into orbit. It was all clouds. Beautiful, swirling clouds, all tinged with scarlet, green, and yellow.

But as *Slave I* descended through the clouds, Boba saw that they were actually made of smoke and steam and toxic gas. The smell was so bad that it even penetrated the ship's systems. The stink was terrible but the colors were beautiful as *Slave I* crossed the line from the dark side of the planet into the light.

Pollution makes for great sunrises.

The smell didn't seem to bother Aurra Sing. Nothing seemed to bother her. "Fly slow and low," she said. It was the first thing she had said in hours. The entire trip from Coruscant had been silent.

That suited Boba fine. He had nothing to say to her, either. She was not his ally but his adversary.

As *Slave I* dropped lower, Boba saw the surface of Raxus Prime for the first time. It was covered with rubble, trash, junk, and garbage, piled in huge twisted heaps and rows like grotesque mountain ranges. Rusted, busted starships, scorched weaponry, mangled machinery, gobs and stacks of glass and steel lay half buried under heaps of slag. And all of it oozed and steamed and smoked, fouling the air above and the water below.

Though it all looked dead, it was alive. Boba saw tiny brown-robed creatures scurrying through the oily wasteland. He saw birds the color of dirt, like smears against the sky. There were no cities, but every few kilometers a smokestack belching fumes marked the site of a refinery or recycling plant, run by scurrying oil-smeared droids.

"Slower, kid."

Aurra Sing consulted a code on her wristwatch. "It should be along here somewhere. Look for a lopsided hill and a lake — there it is!"

The "hill" was a heap of foul refuse a thousand meters high. Twisted, leafless, mutant trees grew from its ravaged slopes, fed by the continual rain that oozed from the stinking clouds.

The "lake" was a pool of iridescent liquid the color of bile. Following Aurra Sing's instructions, Boba set the ship down on a flat spot between the lake and the base of the hill.

"Don't shut it off."

"Huh?"

"The ship. Leave it running. I'm getting out of here. You're staying. This is it."

"You can't leave me here! You can't steal my ship!" said Boba.

"Who says? The ship is my pay," said Aurra Sing. She opened the hatch and lowered the ramp. "There is a door in the side of the hill. As soon as I leave, it will open for you. My client is waiting for you inside. Don't forget your flight bag."

She tossed it out, onto the stinking, steaming "ground." Boba ran after it. She closed the ramp behind him.

"You can't just leave me here!" Boba yelled, banging on the hull of the ship. "I'll run away!"

"Look around — I don't think so!" she yelled back. "I'm gone. Good luck, Boba Fett. I hope you can live up to your father's reputation. He was the genuine article. Who knows, maybe someday you will be, too. I liked the way you handled that bartender."

Boba could hardly believe it. She had rescued him, then betrayed him, then robbed him, and then complimented him! And now she was about to leave him alone on the foulest planet in the galaxy. He banged on the hatch in a rage, but instead of opening, it sealed with a hiss.

He felt truly alone now. There was no one he could trust.

Slave I's engines whined. Boba knew that sound. He stepped back, out of the way. He watched helplessly as the starship — *his* starship! — rose into the noxious clouds and disappeared.

Once again, he felt dangerously close to tears. At the same time, he could barely breathe. Suddenly, he heard a sound behind him.

He turned. A door in the hillside was sliding open. Inside, Boba could see a brightly lighted hall, leading to a carpeted stairway.

Boba didn't wait to be invited. Coughing and gagging, he ran inside.

Now what? Boba thought as the door slid shut.

Before he had a chance to answer his own question, he heard a voice behind him. "Welcome to Raxus Prime, Boba Fett."

The voice was familiar. So were the lean, lined face and the hawklike eyes.

"Count Tyranus! I mean, Count Dooku!"

"You are among friends now, Boba," said the Count. "You can call me anything you please. Count will do."

"My father told me to find you," said Boba.

"And I made sure it happened," said the Count. "I see that Aurra Sing did a superb job and delivered you here safely."

"Yes, sir," said Boba. "I mean, no, sir. You see, she stole my ship, and it's . . ."

The Count smiled and raised his hand. "Don't worry. Your ship is safe. Everything will be fine from now on. You must be very tired."

Boba nodded. It was true.

"Don't worry about a thing," said the Count, placing his cold hand on Boba's head. "Come, let me show you to your room. Let me carry your bag."

Boba followed him up the long stairs. The carpets were deep and soft. Who would have imagined that there was such an elegant palace on the planet of garbage? Even the air was sweet. There was only a very faint foul smell from the planet outside.

"I have big plans for you, Boba," said the Count. "Plans that would have made your father proud. But first you need to rest. You must be tired after all your travels."

Boba nodded. He had packed a lot of adventures into just a few days. The escape from the Jedi starfighter on Geonosis, the escape from the Jedi woman back on Kamino, the recovery of his ship and the robbery gone wrong on the moons of Bogden, the struggle with the bartender on Coruscant . . .

He had lost the ship, but he would get it back. The Count had promised, hadn't he? Something like that.

A lot of stuff for a ten-year-old, he realized. He *was* tired. But he was also confused. He knew he should be happy. He had been lucky. He had completed the first part of his quest. He had found Tyranus. Now he would find Wisdom.

So why had he felt a cold chill when the Count put his hand on top of his head?

Probably just nerves, Boba thought as he followed the Count up the stairs, toward his room.

And his unknown future.